THE MYSTERY ON OBSERVATORY HILL

Eleanor Rosellini

emmis
books

For further information, contact the publisher at

Emmis Books
1700 Madison Road
Cincinnati, OH 45206
www.emmisbooks.com

Library of Congress Cataloging-in-Publication Data

Rosellini, Eleanor Florence.
  The mystery on Observatory Hill / by Eleanor Rosellini.
    p. cm.
  Summary: In Germany with their parents, a sister and brother uncover a mystery at the Hamburg Observatory.
  ISBN 1-57860-235-1
  [1. Brothers and sisters--Fiction. 2. Scientists--Fiction. 3. Astronomical observatories--Fiction. 4. Hamburg (Germany)--Fiction. 5. Germany--Fiction. 6. Mystery and detective stories.] I. Title.
  PZ7.R71862Mys 2005
  [Fic]--dc22
                                        2005005992

All characters and events portrayed in this story are fictional.

Edited by Jessica Yerega
Cover art by Heather Mingo
Designed by Andrea Kupper

WITH SPECIAL THANKS TO THE SCIENTISTS AND STAFF
OF THE HAMBURG OBSERVATORY, WHOSE HOSPITALITY
DURING MY FAMILY'S MAGICAL SUMMER STAY AT THE
GUESTHOUSE IS WARMLY REMEMBERED.

DEN MITARBEITERN DER HAMBURGER STERNWARTE
DANKE ICH HERZLICH FÜR IHRE GASTFREUNDSCHAFT
WÄHREND UNSERES ANGENEHMEN AUFENTHALTS IM
GÄSTEHAUS.

Observatory Hill

Hamburg

Berlin

GERMANY

Munich

TABLE OF CONTENTS

Chapter 1: A Shadow in the Moonlight............7

Chapter 2: Interesting Discoveries...................13

Chapter 3: Elizabeth Meets Her Match............22

Chapter 4: A Midnight Adventure...................34

Chapter 5: Investigating the Scene...................43

Chapter 6: A Long Night..................................52

Chapter 7: Trouble!...62

Chapter 8: The Mysterious Stranger.................70

Chapter 9: Another Trap..................................77

Chapter 10: Peter's Proof of Courage...............86

Chapter 11: The Pendulum Swings...................96

Chapter 12: The Pirates' Den..........................102

Chapter 13: A Ghostly Tale............................110

Chapter 14: Down in the Dungeon.................117

Chapter 15: Hidden Treasure.........................126

Afterword: Be a World Explorer.....................130

The dim haze of mystery brings old and new together.

CHAPTER 1

A Shadow in the Moonlight

"Them! ...Them! ... They're everywhere! ... All over!"

Them? Elizabeth Pollack, ace detective, forced her eyes open and lifted her head off the pillow. She peered into the dim light. Across the room her brother Jonathan sat up in bed, muttering like a madman.

"Them!" He swung his arms, pointing wildly in all directions. Then, like a tree falling in the forest, he dropped back onto his pillow and mumbled himself back to sleep.

Elizabeth propped herself up on her elbow and gazed around the room. Nothing made sense. For one thing, what was Jonathan doing in here? And for another—she felt her face—why was she wearing her glasses in the middle of the night? She stared for a moment at the high ceiling, then sat up stiffly in a narrow, unfamiliar bed. She found herself in a large room milky with moonlight. White walls, simple furniture, and in the middle of the floor, two large suitcases. Now everything slipped back into place—the cramped, sleepless night on the airplane, the landing in Hamburg, and finally, the taxi ride to the white stone house on Observatory Hill. Elizabeth felt her shoulders relax. Germany. Of course. They were in Germany.

The pale green face of her travel clock showed just past midnight. The last thing Elizabeth remembered was unpacking her suitcase and reading a book in bed. She must have been ...

"Where's the soap? Where's the stick?" Jonathan began mumbling again as he turned over in bed. Elizabeth looked at her brother and gave a long sigh. Jonathan was eight years old, and he never did anything quietly, not even sleep. Sharing a room with him for a month was definitely going to be annoying.

Elizabeth tried to go back to sleep, but her eyes popped open every time she forced them shut. Finally, she gave up. She slipped out of bed and climbed up on a chair in front of a row of high windows. These were the kind of German windows she loved—the ones that opened into the room like little doors. Swinging open the middle window, she propped her elbows on the sill and leaned out into the darkness.

Midnight on Observatory Hill was like nothing Elizabeth had ever seen. Great, dark trees stood hushed against the sky. Silvery paths cut narrow ribbons through the grass. And at the end of each path, a domed observatory gleamed as white as a full moon.

Elizabeth took a deep breath, feeling the night pour over her. She had to remind herself it was summer. At home, in Indiana, August nights were jungle hot and noisy with insects. But here it was cool. And so still.

If Elizabeth hadn't been a detective she might not have noticed the flicker of light in the distance. Beyond the last path, by a row of tall hedges, a tiny flame burst into life, then disappeared. A match, perhaps, or a cigarette lighter. Elizabeth leaned farther out the window, peering into the night. She could see something else now. A single dark figure stopped for a moment, then hurried along the hedge and out of sight. She kept her eyes on the bushes, her mind taking off like a race car. Why was someone walking by the hedge instead of on the smooth, lighted path? Did he, or she, not want to be seen? And why was . . . ? Suddenly Elizabeth jerked her head back inside. She had heard a rumbling sound, shivering through the darkness like a moan. She stared at the large observatory just across the path. The dome was moving!

"Huh? Wuhwaszat?" Jonathan sat up in bed again, this time fully awake.

"It's the observatory," whispered Elizabeth. "The roof just opened up." She pointed out the window. The two halves of the dome had slid to the side, making a large dark opening in the middle. "They must be using the telescope. Just think, Jon, they could be looking at Mars or Jupiter."

"Maybe. But I'm hungry." Jonathan swung his legs over the side of the bed. "And I can't go back to sleep unless I get something to eat."

Elizabeth didn't even try to argue, and besides, for some reason she was hungry too. With Jonathan behind her, she tiptoed to the bedroom door and pushed down the handle.

"Don't make any noise, Jon. We're not supposed to be up." She stepped into a wide hallway and stared into the darkness at four white doors. The one straight ahead, she remembered, led down the stairs and out the front door of the guesthouse. On the left were the doors to the bathroom and the other bedroom. She pushed open the fourth door.

"Mom! How come you're up?"

Mrs. Pollack, with a sweatshirt over her long nightgown, sat at a small kitchen table heaped with food. "Oh, great! Two more hungry people who can't sleep! Your father's the only one still in bed." Mrs. Pollack softly shut the kitchen door and the three sat down to a hearty midnight snack—crispy rolls, yogurt with fruit, and dark German bread with butter and jam.

Jonathan got right down to business, eating his way from one end of the table to the other. Finally, he stood up and dusted a shower of bread crumbs from his pajamas. "I'm not tired anymore. Can I go outside?"

"Of course not," laughed Mrs. Pollack. "It's the middle of the night."

"But it's weird," said Elizabeth. "I'm not tired either. Except I feel like everything inside me is turned upside down. Because of the time change, right, Mom?"

"Exactly. Germany is in a different time zone, so it's seven hours later here than it is at home. Your body is still on Indiana time, so you feel like it's ..." she glanced at her watch, "about five thirty in the afternoon. You'll be sleeping late for a couple days, but after that you'll get used to the new time. Just like when we were in Germany a few years ago."

Jonathan plopped back down on his chair. "Well, sometime I wanna go see that big telescope. We just heard the dome opening up."

"I know," said Mrs. Pollack. "I heard it, too. I was just reading about all the observatories here. There are twelve of them, and the one that just opened is the biggest." She cleared a spot among the yogurt containers and opened a booklet. "Here's a picture of what's on the inside. The telescope is called the Big Refractor. It was made a long time ago—in 1912."

"It's beautiful," said Elizabeth. The telescope in the picture was long and slender, like a pirate's spyglass that grew bigger and bigger until it could see all the way to the stars.

"Do you think they'd let us look through it, Mom?" asked Jonathan.

"I'm not sure. We're only staying here because it's a guesthouse for the University. The history project I'm working on doesn't have anything to do with the observatories."

"But Dad's a science teacher," said Elizabeth. "And astronomy is a science."

"Well, if I know your father, he'll figure out some way to get us into the observatory. But right now, let's get back to bed." Mrs. Pollack followed the two into their room and closed the heavy brown curtains. "You can read if you're not sleepy, but just make sure to keep the curtains closed. The light from the windows can interfere with the telescopes." She left the room, then popped her head in again. "And remember to walk quietly. The woman who runs the guesthouse lives in the apartment below us. I'm sure she's sleeping."

"Wait, Jon, don't turn on the light. I have to check something."

Elizabeth parted the curtains and leaned in toward the window. She heard low voices, then saw a man and a woman, both carrying briefcases, headed toward the Big Refractor. Astronomers, Elizabeth thought. The woman unlocked a small side door and the two disappeared into the observatory. After the door clicked shut, Observatory Hill fell back into silence. Slowly Elizabeth swept her gaze back and forth along the dark row of hedges. She saw no sign of the mysterious person she had seen earlier.

"Hey, Elizabeth. There's a lady who never cuts her toenails. And they just keep growing and growing. And now they're really, really long."

Elizabeth clenched her teeth. She knew what Jonathan was reading. *The Encyclopedia of the Totally Disgusting* was her brother's favorite book. Or more exactly, his favorite instrument for torturing his sister. Maybe when they were ready to leave Germany the book could be— accidentally—left behind on the wrong side of the Atlantic Ocean.

"And her toenails got so long they started curling and twisting. And she can't wear regular shoes anymore. She has to lift her feet when she moves, like when you walk on the beach with flippers. Wanna see the picture? It's a close-up."

Elizabeth turned to see Jonathan on his bed with a flashlight. She unclenched her teeth and managed to talk him into a game of cards. "Here, Jon. You deal and I'll put your book on the floor." Elizabeth sat down facing Jonathan. One tap of her heel sent *The Encyclopedia of the Totally Disgusting* far underneath the bed.

After half an hour, Jonathan pushed his pile of cards into the middle. "You win, Elizabeth. I'm tired." He flopped down and pulled up the quilt.

Elizabeth settled into her own bed but still couldn't sleep. "Jonathan," she whispered, "what if we can't speak German anymore? I mean, we've been reading lots of books in German, but we haven't been speaking it."

"Oh, don't worry. Dad says we just have to start talking and then we'll ... And anyway... " Jonathan rolled over and finished his sentence with a light snore.

Elizabeth laid back and closed her eyes. She thought about the last time they were in Germany. They had come for a whole year—second grade for her and kindergarten for Jonathan. She had felt so much at home in Germany then, but that was three years ago. Now everything felt strange and new again.

She reached into her backpack and pulled out a thick leather book with gold letters fading on the cover. *How to Think Like a Detective.* She read it every night before she went to sleep. She could practically recite it line by line. As Elizabeth opened the book, a tiny white piece of paper fluttered to the floor. Picking it up, she remembered the old Chinese man selling cookies at the airport. "A special fortune cookie, just for you," he had said. Elizabeth gazed at the strange fortune she had found inside: *The dim haze of mystery brings old and new together.*

It was past three in the morning when Elizabeth finally turned off the light. She listened for a time to the unfamiliar sounds—muffled footsteps and low voices, doors opening and closing as the astronomers went about their work. Even with her eyes closed, she could imagine the white domes of the observatories, gleaming against the nighttime sky. And one lone figure hurrying along a dark hedge.

Elizabeth knew that Observatory Hill was a place of science, but there was something more. Something magical and ... she floated off to sleep on the last word that came to her mind ... mysterious.

CHAPTER 2

INTERESTING DISCOVERIES

Twenty minutes after eleven? Elizabeth sat up in bed, squinting at her travel clock. She had never slept so late in her life. The curtains were already drawn back. A stream of sunshine told her the day was up and running.

Elizabeth put on her glasses and sat up. Jonathan's bed was empty. She could see he had been busy unpacking. His treasures, compliments of Jack's Joke Shop, were lined up reverently on his night table. Fake cockroach. Plastic ice cube with a fly inside. Whoopee cushion. Skeleton hand. Rubber vomit, large and small. *The Encyclopedia of the Totally Disgusting* had been found and put in a place of honor on his pillow. Elizabeth pulled the covers over her head.

"So how's the world traveler this morning? Probably feeling some disturbance in your biological rhythms." Elizabeth peeked out to see her father, tall and thin, standing in the doorway. She could tell she was about to have a science lesson. "You know, we all have an inner clock. It's our bodies' way of telling us what time of day it is. But when we travel to a new time zone, our inner clock doesn't match the new time. Then we feel something called jet lag."

"Yeah, our bodies think it's 4:20 a.m.," announced Jonathan. "My watch is still set on Indiana time."

"Oh, don't remind me of Indiana time. Let's just have breakfast, or lunch, or whatever it is." Elizabeth pulled herself out of bed. "Where's Mom?"

"She's already at the University, meeting with someone," said Mr. Pollack. "The rest of us won't be going anywhere today. You two can just take it easy."

After a quick breakfast, Elizabeth and Jonathan set out exploring. The cool night had softened into a gentle summer day. Elizabeth took off her sweatshirt and tied it around her waist.

"So where should we start?" She stood in front of the guesthouse, hesitating. Everything around her looked so ... grand. The trees were tall and straight, stretching their wide arms over shady lawns. Elizabeth could see the Big Refractor Observatory up close now. It stood before her as solemn as a temple, with two white pillars guarding a set of giant wooden doors. As the doors swung open from the inside, Elizabeth half expected to see someone wearing a toga and carrying scrolls. But the figure that hurried down the steps wore a short-sleeved shirt and carried a neat stack of papers.

"I'm going to make a map," announced Jonathan. "To improve my powers of observation." He settled on a bench across from the guesthouse and balanced a large sketch pad on his lap.

"You're going to *sit*? And make a map?" Elizabeth walked over and gave him a cautious smile. Maybe his detective training was paying off after all. She sat down on the bench—carefully—just in case her brother had any idea of sneaking a whoopee cushion underneath her. But Jonathan was already busy with his map. He started with the entrance gate and the small guardhouse. He added a stick figure guard and a car checking in. A double line, not quite straight, was the narrow roadway that ran in front of the bench where they were sitting. The guesthouse was easy to sketch—a simple, boxy house with a pointed roof, like the first house every child draws. Jonathan stared at a large stone building with two long rows of windows. On the sign in front was a long German word that meant *Administration Building*.

"Here, Elizabeth, I'm not so good at drawing. You finish it." Jonathan bounded off, heading across the street to a path that ran along the side of the guesthouse. The back garden was hidden by a hedge, but he soon found a small hole in the bushes. He stood on tiptoe to peek in.

"Oh, gross!" Jonathan cooed with delight. "You gotta see this, Elizabeth!" He ran back and pulled his sister to the opening in the hedge. Elizabeth rolled her eyes. If there was anything weird to be found, Jonathan could sniff it out like a bloodhound. At first she saw nothing unusual—just sheets hanging on a clothesline and two chairs under an apple tree. And then ... of course. In the back of the garden was a small fish pond, and next to it, a statue of a pudgy little boy. Elizabeth laughed. A stream of water came from the statue, as if the boy were peeing into the pond.

"I don't know how you always find this stuff, Jon." Elizabeth tugged her brother's arm. "Anyway. Let's get going. I want to find the other observatories. Mom said there are twelve."

Jonathan skipped ahead down a smooth path of hard-packed sand. They had nearly reached one of the small observatories when a young man in a green work suit came out of a storage building. He looked at them, then walked in their direction.

Jonathan stopped and backed up a few steps. "Oh, no. He's probably going to tell us we're not supposed to be here."

"I don't know what he's going to say," said Elizabeth. "All I know is, we're going to have to speak German."

To her relief, the man smiled and waved as he approached. He certainly looked friendly enough. And he was wearing a Chicago Cubs baseball hat.

"Guten Tag, Kinder. Ihr seid bestimmt unsere amerikanischen Gäste."[1]

Elizabeth hesitated for a moment, then plunged into German. "Yes, we are the American visitors. We are staying at the guesthouse. One

---

[1] "Good day, children. You must be our American guests."

month. My name is Elizabeth, and my brother's name is Jonathan."

The man gave them both a quick, firm handshake. He spoke in a slow clear German that was easy to understand. "And my name is Karl. I take care of the grounds here on Observatory Hill. Come on, I'll give you a tour." He seemed to notice Jonathan staring at his baseball cap. "A cousin in Chicago," explained Karl. "A big fan of American baseball." Karl showed them a building with a ping-pong table, then took them to a field where they could play soccer. The rules were simple. They could go anywhere, as long as they weren't noisy around the buildings where the scientists were working. Elizabeth relaxed. Speaking German felt strange, but comfortable too—like putting on a pair of old shoes she hadn't worn in a long time.

Karl stood with them at the edge of the field. "And your parents don't have to worry about you getting lost. There's a fence around the whole complex."

"What's that over there?" asked Jonathan. "On the other side of those big trees." Elizabeth followed Jonathan's gaze. In the distance a round brick tower rose up. A fairy tale tower, with long, narrow windows and a black roof pointed like a wizard's cap.

"That's our town castle. It's been rebuilt a few times, but the oldest part is seven hundred years old."

"Elizabeth," whispered Jonathan. "How do you say *dungeon* in German?" Elizabeth shrugged her shoulders. Jonathan turned to Karl. "Are there ... rooms under the castle, and maybe some skeletons and rats?"

Karl laughed. "A dungeon, you mean? Oh, yes, there is a dungeon. But no skeletons as far as I know."

He turned to leave. "Just one more thing. I'm sure you'll be meeting Peter Hoffmann. His parents work in the library here. He's about your age, Elizabeth. Eleven, I think. Everybody here knows Peter. He's ... Well, he's ..." Karl took off his cap and wiped his brow.

"He's one of a kind, you might say. You'll like him."

After Karl left, Jonathan and Elizabeth walked from one end of Observatory Hill to the other. Following a maze of shady paths, they discovered ten more observatories, all white, domed buildings much like the Big Refractor, but not as big. They ended up back at the sports field. "There must be one more observatory, Jon. Mom said there were twelve. Maybe we could ..."

"I think it's a buckeye!" Jonathan took off into a patch of high grass, following the zigzag path of a bright butterfly.

"Hey, Elizabeth, I found something. You gotta see it."

Elizabeth tried to glare suspiciously at her brother, but she couldn't see him. She marched stiffly through the unmowed grass, preparing herself for anything. A rat hole. A nest of snakes. "Jonathan?" She squeezed between two fat bushes, yanking their prickly fingers out of her hair. On the other side, she could feel a path under her feet, but it was uneven and messy with weeds. The trees were taller here, their branches woven into a high, green ceiling. The place felt lonely and quiet, like a room that had been locked up for a long time.

"See, I told you I found something. Right there." Jonathan pointed to a tangle of bushes and trees. Underneath, a long low building sat half hidden in the leaves. Its metal roof was rounded, like a barrel cut in half the long way. Elizabeth took a few steps closer. A track with rusty steel wheels stretched along the bottom edge of the roof.

"So what is it?" asked Jonathan.

Elizabeth stretched herself tall and looked down on her brother. "Elementary, my dear Watson. This does not resemble the other buildings. Observe, however. The roof is divided into two parts. The wheels are used to open the roof. I therefore conclude that this building is the twelfth observatory." Jonathan had already tried to run away, but Elizabeth had a firm grip on his shoulder. "Observe, Dr. Watson, the large branches hanging down on the roof. I conclude that this observatory has not been used in a very long time. And furthermore ... uh, furthermore ..." Elizabeth looked around while Jonathan squirmed, "the weeds on the path tell me that few people come here at all."

Jonathan shook himself loose and rewarded Elizabeth's lecture by sticking out his tongue. "Let's keep looking around," he said, "but cut out that Dr. Watson stuff." The two walked along the side of the building, peeking where they could through the dense coat of bushes. Around the corner, at the narrow end of the building, the bushes had been cleared away. Five wooden steps led to a wide metal door. Across from the stairway was another building, much smaller and made of gray stone.

"It's like a little stone box," said Elizabeth. She took the sketch pad from Jonathan and made a rough drawing of the tiny stone building, including the small columns on either side of the entrance. The place was a perfect gloomy match for the old observatory. Hidden from the sun, the stone walls had turned dark and spotty, like gravestones in an old burial ground. A rusty padlock and boarded-up window scarred the wooden door.

"*Meridian.*" Elizabeth copied down the word that was deeply carved into the stone above the door. "That must be the name of the observatory. We'll have to ask Dad what it means."

She stepped back onto the path and looked around. They couldn't walk any farther. A wrought-iron fence, like a row of long black spears, marked the end of the observatory grounds. Beyond the fence a wide sandy path led straight to the castle. Elizabeth could see it clearly now, the black-roofed towers and the strong deep red of the bricks.

"I'm gonna try the door to the observatory." Jonathan ran up the wooden stairs, then clattered back down without stopping. "Uh ... maybe not."

Elizabeth looked up at the metal door. The Meridian Observatory couldn't have had a better guard. The latch was protected by a web stretching from one side of the door to the other. In the middle sat a monster of a spider—black and fat—the kind that looked like it could have someone's little finger for lunch.

Jonathan and Elizabeth decided not to stay any longer. They found their way back to the guesthouse and spent a quiet afternoon. Jonathan was still tired from their long trip, and even took a nap. Elizabeth sat on her bed with her red spiral detective notebook in her lap. The book was already half full, with page after page of notes on the two mysteries they had solved. *The Puzzle in the Portrait. The Mystery of the Ancient Coins.*

Elizabeth was tempted to write something about the Meridian Observatory. She had found out one thing. A meridian was an imaginary line passing from the north pole to the south pole, like longitude. But Elizabeth didn't want to write anything about their discovery. Not yet, anyway. It wasn't a mystery. Just a question. Why was one observatory overgrown and abandoned, when all the others were so neat and well-kept? Elizabeth was sure the Meridian Observatory had a story to tell. She was determined to find out what it was.

They had a late dinner that night, finishing up the dishes at nine thirty. Elizabeth and Jonathan used the last bit of daylight to go to the soccer field. Elizabeth felt full of energy, blasting in three goals past Jonathan's dives. Then suddenly she stopped. The air was perfectly still now, quiet with the glow that comes just before the night rushes in. Elizabeth glanced across the field of tall grass. She couldn't see the Meridian Observatory, but she knew it was there, dark and lonely, behind the dim line of trees.

"Let's get going, Jon. Before it gets dark." Jonathan tucked the ball under his arm, and they hurried along the curved paths toward the guesthouse. The lights were on in two of the observatories, and the dome of the Big Refractor was open again.

Mr. Pollack was sitting on the bench across from the guesthouse. Elizabeth and Jonathan started to walk toward him, but hesitated when they saw he was talking to someone.

"Come over here," called Mr. Pollack. "I want you to meet Professor Bergstrom." They were introduced to an elderly man with thin, white hair. He spoke a careful, correct English in an accent Elizabeth didn't recognize.

"Professor Bergstrom is from Sweden," explained Mr. Pollack. "He's retired now, but he worked as an astronomer here for over forty years."

Jonathan gave his sister a jab on the arm. "Ask him."

"Well, uh, could we ask you a few questions about the Meridian Observatory?"

"Ah, so you've discovered the Meridian. What would you like to know?"

"Well, mostly," said Elizabeth, "we were wondering why the observatory is so … so lonely and hidden away."

Professor Bergstrom nodded slowly. He had the palest blue eyes, thought Elizabeth, like the morning sky just as the sun comes up.

"Yes, I can tell you that. You see, a long time ago a famous astronomer named Heinrich Vollrath worked in that observatory. His telescope, the Meridian, was used to map the exact position of stars in the northern sky. And then about sixty years ago the telescope was sent to Australia and was used to study the southern skies. You know, in its day, the Meridian telescope was one of the finest in the world, but now it's too old to be of use. I believe it was taken apart and stored in a museum somewhere. So the building you discovered is an observatory without a telescope. For many years now the observatory and the little building next to it have been used for storage."

Elizabeth shrugged her shoulders. "I guess it's not so mysterious after all."

Professor Bergstrom leaned forward, his pale eyes lost in the darkness. "Not mysterious? Oh, but you're wrong, young lady. Very wrong." The professor's words, spoken in his Swedish accent, rose and dipped in a pleasant singsong, like a boat rocking on gentle waves. "Yes, we have much here that is interesting. Mystery. Ghost stories too. And now I will tell you the most important secret. You see … there's something quite extraordinary about Observatory Hill." Professor Bergstrom lifted his gaze upwards. Silently he studied the first glimmer of stars peeking out of the night sky. Finally, he looked down again. "Treasure," he said slowly. "Hidden treasure."

CHAPTER 3

ELIZABETH MEETS HER MATCH

Treasure. The word set Jonathan off like a firecracker. He began a wild dance around the nearest tree. Elizabeth sighed. She *was* going to tell Professor Bergstrom that they were detectives—real detectives—but real detectives don't run around trees every time they get excited.

Professor Bergstrom followed Jonathan's leaps with a puzzled smile. "Don't worry," said Elizabeth. "It's just the Outer Mongolian Warrior Dance. He always does it when he gets excited. But anyway, don't say anything else about the mystery until I get back. Please." Elizabeth rushed across the empty street and flew up the stairs to the second floor apartment. Her mother sat in the tiny kitchen pecking away at a laptop computer.

"Hi, Mom. We have a mystery—maybe. Gotta go." She was back outside in less than a minute, clutching the tools of her trade. Lucky green pen. Red spiral detective notebook. Flashlight. She caught Jonathan by the shoulder in mid-leap.

"Quit being weird and do something useful." She handed Jonathan the flashlight. "Hold this over the page while I write." She sat cross-legged on the grass and looked up at Professor Bergstrom. "What kind of treasure?"

22

"Well, it is not what you think," he said. "There are no diamonds, or gold, or silver. This is ... " he looked up again to the stars, "a scientific treasure."

"A scientific treasure?"

"Yes. A great scientific treasure. And it has to do with Professor Vollrath and the Meridian Observatory you find so mysterious. You see, when Professor Vollrath used the Meridian telescope to study the stars, he wrote down his observations in notebooks. His last two notebooks, from the years 1918 and 1919, were hidden and have never been found. Hundreds of pages of scientific data have been lost to the world."

"You mean, *he* hid the notebooks?" asked Jonathan. "But why?"

Professor Bergstrom sat down on the bench next to Mr. Pollack. "I must tell you that Professor Vollrath was an odd man. A man very much alone. He had always taken his notebooks to the library for safekeeping. But about two years before his death, he stopped doing this. Instead, he began keeping his notebooks with him at all times. When he had to leave Observatory Hill, he hid them. In the winter of 1919, the professor went on holiday. As usual, he hid his notes before leaving. But this time he never returned. That was the year of the Spanish influenza. A terrible epidemic. The professor fell ill while he was away and died without telling anyone where his notebooks were hidden. For many years people searched for his notes, but they were never found." Professor Bergstrom made a sweeping motion through the darkness. "They remain hidden to this day. Somewhere on Observatory Hill. Of course now they've almost been forgotten. Only the old ones like me even know the notes were lost."

Elizabeth stopped writing. "But wasn't there anyone who knew where the hiding place was?"

Professor Bergstrom shook his head. "No one was ever told. But there is one clue. May I?" He reached out for Elizabeth's notebook and wrote something. Jonathan shined the flashlight down on the page. At the bottom were three dots, close together and in the form of a triangle.

"But I don't get it," said Elizabeth.

"I also have puzzled over this," said the professor. "It is said that whenever Professor Vollrath was asked about the hiding place, he would answer by drawing this symbol on a piece of paper. Other than that, he would say nothing. No one understands this strange drawing. Three dots. What could it mean?"

Elizabeth couldn't see her father's face in the darkness, but she could imagine his eyebrows raised in a doubtful arch. He was a science teacher, a hunter of facts. And the fact was that they had never solved a mystery with so little to go on. Three dots on a piece of paper.

"So there's no other clue?" she asked.

"I have no other information. But there is a display about Professor Vollrath in the library. Right over there in the Administration Building. You might want to look at it. Of course, this is a very old mystery and perhaps not so exciting for young people today."

Elizabeth nudged Jonathan's arm. The professor didn't know it, but they liked nothing better than solving old mysteries from the past, mysteries everyone else had forgotten.

Professor Bergstrom rose stiffly from the bench. In the distance the sound of a motor chopped at the quiet night.

"Didn't you say something about ghost stories?" asked Jonathan.

"Oh, yes. Of course. There are people who say that he ..." The end of Professor Bergstrom's sentence was drowned out by the thumping beat of a helicopter. It swooped over the observatories, then leaned into a slow arc toward the castle. In the dim glow of the running lights,

Elizabeth could see the word *Polizei*—"police"—in dark letters on the side. When she looked down again, the professor was waving at a man about to enter the Big Refractor. "I must be going now," he said quickly. "The ghost stories will have to wait for another time."

Just before midnight Elizabeth laid her red detective notebook on the table next to her bed. She had read through all the notes scribbled in the darkness and had written everything over again. Jonathan, in the bed across the room, was already mumbling in his sleep. But Elizabeth had given up even closing her eyes. All she could see were the three mysterious dots, as if they were written on the inside of her eyelids.

An hour later Elizabeth fluffed up her pillow for the fourth time. She stared hard into the darkness until her eyes fell shut on their own. Slowly, the three dots faded away.

At eight in the morning, Elizabeth rolled over and checked the clock. She deserved one more day of jet lag, she decided. She promptly fell asleep again—a lively morning sleep, with dreams tumbling in one after the other. All the events of yesterday came back, but all mixed up, like a piece of paper torn to bits and tossed in the wind. She dreamed of an old man in a toga sitting on the steps of the Meridian Observatory. He smiled at her in a kind way, holding up a tiny telescope, then … the telescope became a garden hose and the old man was squirting her right in the face.

As soon as Elizabeth's eyes opened, she realized she was wet. Real-life water dripped down the side of her nose and made a wet patch on her pillow. As she sat up in bed, another stream of water hit her square on the chin.

"Jonathan!" She saw him with a green squirt gun, snickering behind the bedroom door. Elizabeth tore out of bed. The chase was on. Within five minutes Mr. Pollack had sent both of them to separate rooms. Jonathan was in trouble for waking up his sister with a squirt gun. Elizabeth was scolded for throwing Jonathan's rubber vomit out the window, where it was run over by a maintenance truck.

As soon as the time-out was over, Jonathan rushed out the door and stomped down the stairs.

"I'm going to play soccer. Alone!"

"And I'm going to work on our case. Alone!" called Elizabeth out the window. She could see two workmen having an early lunch on the lawn, and a group of scientists walking along the paths toward the observatories.

Elizabeth pulled on a rumpled pair of shorts and a T-shirt. She didn't like getting up late. The whole world was way ahead of her. Her mother had taken an early bus to a library in the city. Her father had set up a little table on the balcony and was looking through some papers.

With a thick slice of dark bread in one hand and her pen in the other, Elizabeth sat at the kitchen table. She turned to a clean, new page in her detective notebook and began to write.

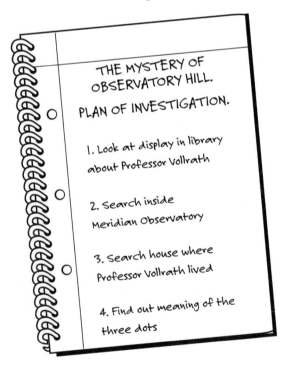

THE MYSTERY OF OBSERVATORY HILL.
PLAN OF INVESTIGATION.

1. Look at display in library about Professor Vollrath

2. Search inside Meridian Observatory

3. Search house where Professor Vollrath lived

4. Find out meaning of the three dots

The fat capital letters looked important on the page, but the list underneath was only four numbers long. Elizabeth had been excited about the mystery the night before, but now she was as doubtful as her father. Three dots weren't much to go on.

She closed the notebook. This will be just for practice, she told herself. And to keep Jonathan away from *The Encyclopedia of the Totally Disgusting*.

"I'm going to the library, Dad," she called. "It's in the Administration Building. And after that, I *might* try to find Jonathan."

Elizabeth walked across the street to the large stone building. She had to put down her notebook and use both hands to pull open the heavy wooden doors. Once inside, she found herself in a cool, dim corridor. She padded down the hall until she came to a set of double doors on the left. Stretching up on tiptoe, she peeked through a small round window. She could see a book-lined room with three long tables in the middle. Several heads were bent over open books.

Elizabeth stayed in the hallway, stepping back from the door. Usually she felt at home in libraries, but she could see this one was different. No padded chairs or chapter books. It was a working library, full of serious people and important-looking books. She took a hesitant step forward, then tightened her ponytail, pushed up her glasses, and stepped inside.

The library was one large room that soared up, two stories high, to a distant ceiling. The walls were nothing but books, except for a row of long windows that looked onto a bright garden. As Elizabeth walked into the room, the heavy door behind her closed with a sharp click. Every face lifted and turned in her direction. Suddenly she wished Jonathan were with her. And she wished she weren't wearing her Camp Happy Days T-shirt from Milton, Indiana.

To the right a librarian sat behind a desk—a woman with a friendly, wide-open face and a cap of straight blond hair. Elizabeth made her way toward the desk as if she were reaching for a life ring.

"Excuse me," said Elizabeth in German, "I'm staying at the guesthouse and I'd like to see the ..." She had forgotten the German word for display. "The pictures of Professor Heinrich Vollrath, please."

"Of course. Follow me." The librarian acted as if it were perfectly natural for an eleven-year-old to be in an astronomy library asking about someone who died over eighty years ago. "It's on the upper level."

Elizabeth followed her up a spiral staircase. A metal walkway high above the floor ran along three walls.

"Here, between these bookcases," said the librarian. "And now I'll leave you to your work." Elizabeth stood before a glass case mounted on the wall. An old black and white photograph labeled *Professor Vollrath, 1915*, showed a small man with a mustache and a short, pointed beard. He stood in front of a brick wall with a large key in one hand and a cigarette in the other. Propped open next to the photo were two narrow notebooks bound in bumpy brown leather. Elizabeth leaned close to the glass to read the words written underneath. *1916. Notes taken by Heinrich Vollrath, astronomer at the Hamburg Observatory.*

What luck, thought Elizabeth. Now she knew exactly what the hidden notebooks looked like. And, somehow, the mystery seemed more real. Maybe the notebooks wouldn't be so hard to find after all. She stared at the display and wrote down a description as best she could, but she couldn't think of much to say. The yellowed pages were full of numbers which had no meaning to her. At the bottom the handwriting was so tiny she couldn't believe a grown man could have written it.

Elizabeth took a look at the last item in the display—a photo of a narrow brick house. She held her breath. If this was Professor Vollrath's house and it gave an address, she and Jonathan could talk to the people who lived there now. Even search the house. She copied down the words.

Das Heinrich-Vollrath-Haus

The home of Heinrich Vollrath. "Oh, no." Elizabeth didn't mean to, but she said the words out loud. She translated into English as she continued writing.

Torn down in 1965 to make way for the new Wolfgang Schmidt Observatory.

Elizabeth turned to her Plan of Investigation and crossed off number three.

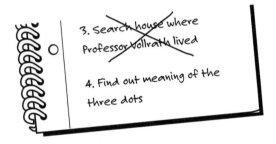

They would never be able to search Professor Vollrath's house. She looked again at the first picture. Professor Vollrath must have been standing in front of the brick wall of his house. A house that didn't exist anymore.

Elizabeth closed her notebook and padded down the spiral staircase. The librarian looked up and smiled.

"Do you have any more information about Professor Vollrath?" asked Elizabeth.

The librarian thought for a moment. "I don't know. Unless … yes, you can try this." She opened her bottom drawer and pulled out a magazine. "This was published on the seventy-fifth anniversary of the opening of Observatory Hill. There's something about Professor Vollrath here." She opened to a page of text with a small picture.

Elizabeth recognized the professor. He was seated at a desk next to a telescope that looked like a smaller version of the Big Refractor.

"You can keep it," said the librarian. "We have plenty. Are you doing a report for school?"

"Not exactly," said Elizabeth. She leaned across the desk. "My brother and I are looking for the notes the professor hid before he died. We're, uh ... well, we're detectives."

One or two heads bobbed up and peered at her.

"And I was wondering if you ever saw anything like this on Observatory Hill," whispered Elizabeth. "It's supposed to be a clue about where the notebooks were hidden." She opened her notebook and showed the drawing of the three dots.

"I'm afraid not," said the librarian. "But you should meet my son Peter." She looked again at the three dots. "Yes, you must definitely meet my son."

Elizabeth left the library with the Observatory Hill magazine tucked into her detective notebook. She would read the article later. Now she headed down the tree-lined path to the soccer field. She wasn't mad at Jonathan any more. How could she be? It was the kind of sunny, just-right summer day when everything—even just walking—felt good.

As Elizabeth neared the soccer field she saw that Jonathan wasn't alone. He was kicking the ball to a wiry boy about her own age. She had a feeling she was about to meet Peter.

The first thing Elizabeth noticed was his hair. She couldn't help but notice it. Elizabeth thought Jonathan's hair was messy, but Peter's seemed to defy the law of gravity. It was cut in a kind of electric shock style, with little blond tufts pointing up to the sky. He stood in front of the goal blocking the shots Jonathan tried to get past him.

"I'll be right back," called Jonathan. He ran up to Elizabeth.

"How do you say *wart* in German?" Elizabeth narrowed her eyes. She didn't know how to say *wart* in German, but even if she did, she would never tell her brother.

"I'm telling him about *The Encyclopedia of the Totally Disgusting.* But I don't know how to say all those words in German."

"Oh, too bad." Elizabeth couldn't hide her smile. "So this is Peter, right, the one Karl talked about. I just met his mother in the library."

"Yeah, he lives in that big house we can see from our balcony. And he really likes to talk."

Peter loped over to the edge of the field. Up close, his sun-pink cheeks gave a hint of freckles. "Peter Hoffmann. Super Sleuth Extraordinaire." He thrust his hand out, and Elizabeth gave him a firm handshake. "Elizabeth Pollack," she answered, raising her chin slightly. "Ace Detective."

Peter's eyebrows rose. "Follow me. Both of you. You're going to see my hide-out." If Elizabeth had been a porcupine, her quills would have stood up and quivered. She had the feeling Peter liked to order people around. They followed him past the soccer field into a wooded area Elizabeth hadn't noticed before. They walked single file down a narrow path. Peter was first in line, yelling back his life story as he walked. He was an only child. His parents both worked at the Astronomy Library, and he had lived on Observatory Hill all his life. He had a complete crime laboratory at home, and he planned to be a police detective. "Technology," he called over his shoulder. "It's all technology."

Peter's German was as fast as a jackhammer. Elizabeth didn't understand everything he said, but maybe that wasn't so bad. She didn't know how much to believe anyway.

At the end of the path, they came to a lean-to made of old boards propped up against a massive tree. "We need another chair," said Peter. He pushed an extra log through the narrow door and the three squeezed inside.

"We're detectives," said Jonathan. "And not just pretend." Peter nodded, obviously unimpressed. Jonathan began talking about the cases he and Elizabeth had worked on—the old note in the portrait, the stolen family treasure, and then their search for ancient gold coins. Peter became more and more excited, and ended up rolling backwards off his log.

"Man, oh man. You really are detectives."

"What kind of cases do you work on?" asked Jonathan.

Peter waved one hand in the air. "Oh … kidnappings, robberies, that kind of thing. I'm investigating a gang of jewel thieves in the city. The villa robberies. It's all over the papers." He leaned back against the tree trunk. "I usually work alone. But if you're as good as you say you are, I *might* let you be my assistants."

Assistants? Elizabeth let out a mighty huff. She had never met anyone like Peter. He reminded her of a frog she had seen in a rainforest book, the kind that swallows air until it blows itself up like a balloon.

"We're working on a mystery too," said Jonathan. "Tell him, Elizabeth."

"Well … " Elizabeth didn't know if Super Sleuth Peter would be interested in finding old scientific notes. "Jon and I like to work on old mysteries, the ones no one else is working on." She opened her detective notebook and read her notes to Peter. He studied the three dots for a long time, but he had no idea what they meant.

"Elizabeth and I want to go back to the Meridian Observatory. That's where Professor Vollrath's telescope was, so we think the notes might be hidden there. You can come along if you want."

"Good idea. Follow me." Peter crawled out of the lean-to and ran down the wooded path and across the soccer field. Elizabeth kept up and managed to pass him just as they came to the tall grass that led to the abandoned observatory.

She was panting hard but was the first to reach the Meridian. She needed to think of something to do—fast. She wasn't going to let Peter start bossing her around. This was her case. And Jonathan's. Quickly she bent down and looked through the keyhole of the tiny stone building next to the observatory.

"You don't have to look through there," said Peter. He pointed to the boarded up window. "Here. This is loose." He slid aside a board nailed to the top of the door. Elizabeth backed away from the gush of damp, musty air. The three took turns looking into the small room, but only the dim outline of tables and chairs could be seen. As for the observatory building itself, the solid metal door offered nothing to spy through, and the spider was still on guard duty.

"I wish we could get inside," said Elizabeth. "We can't see anything from out here."

"Maybe Karl would let us in," said Jonathan.

"Leave it to me," said Peter. "Karl's a good friend of mine. But he's not here today. We'll have to wait until tomorrow to ask him."

Peter crossed his arms and stared at the other two. "I've made a decision. I've had a one-man detective club for too long. You two will be allowed to join."

"Okay," said Jonathan. "Sure."

Elizabeth didn't say anything. She wasn't sure at all.

"But first," said Peter, "You have to prove that you're ready."

"What do you mean, *ready?*" Elizabeth didn't trust the gleam in Peter's eyes.

"It's nothing much," said Peter. "Just a little test." He raised his hands to the sky. "The Peter Hoffmann Super Sleuth Test of Courage … Extraordinaire."

CHAPTER 4

A Midnight Adventure

Test of courage? It sounded to Elizabeth like some kind of stupid boy idea. She struggled to find the right words in German. "If this is about doing something dangerous to show off, you can forget it."

"No. No. Nothing dangerous. You just have to be a little brave, that's all." Peter reached into his pocket and pulled out a long, finger-sized stone. When he held it up, Elizabeth could see it was hollowed out like a tube. "This is my telescope rock. I found it last summer on an island in the North Sea."

"So?" Elizabeth was still suspicious.

"So all you need to do is come here and fetch this. Just the two of you." Peter set the stone on the top step near the door to the abandoned observatory. "When the castle clock strikes twelve." Peter smiled. "Midnight. Or are you afraid to be out alone after dark?"

"I'm not afraid." Jonathan spun around and struck a karate pose.

Elizabeth looked down the long, lonely path leading to the observatory. A light wind stirred the trees, turning the low-hanging branches into quivering hands.

"I'm not afraid either," she said. "It's not that hard."

Jonathan leaped up to the third step. "Midnight on Observatory Hill. The sky is black and stormy. A gang of robbers is hiding behind the Observatory. They attack. Jonathan does the Outer Mongolian Warrior Dance. Then he scares them with his ... with his long, sharp toenails. He gets away, swinging on vines from tree to tree. He throws

34

a … fishing net over the whole gang. He takes them to the dungeon in the castle. And they all have to sit on whoopee cushions and eat chocolate-covered grasshoppers and … "

"Jon? Hello?" Elizabeth waved her hand in front of her brother's face. "First we have to figure out how to talk Mom and Dad into letting us go out alone at midnight."

"You'll think of something," said Peter. "So here's what you do. You grab the stone, then you go back to the guesthouse and send me an e-mail."

"Send you an e-mail?" asked Elizabeth. "But you live right next door to the guesthouse. And anyway, we're not even set up for e-mail. Can't we just stand on the sidewalk and wave up at your window?"

Peter puffed himself up. "Technology," he said, "is the future of crime detection. But if you want, we can go low-tech." He tapped his fingertips together, then nodded. "When you get back, go out on your balcony and signal with a flashlight. I'll watch from my bedroom window. Ten seconds of short blinks if you get the stone; three long blinks if you don't have it. If you want to meet me tomorrow, make a circle with the flashlight, then blink the time. I'll blink back four times so you know I got the message. *Verstanden?*"

"Of course I understand." Elizabeth repeated the instructions to herself. She had never heard anything so complicated.

She glanced up through the trees and saw her father walking across the soccer field. Elizabeth looked at her watch.

"I think Dad's looking for us, Jon. I forgot to tell you. He wants us to go shopping with him and help carry groceries. We have to catch the bus."

"Can't Mom go with him?" groaned Jonathan.

"She's at the library in the city. So we have to help. Dad can't carry all the stuff alone." Elizabeth waved her arms and hurried down the path.

"Just remember," yelled Peter. "Don't start out until you hear the castle clock strike twelve."

Elizabeth didn't want to think too much about wandering around at midnight. She was glad to be distracted by a trip into town. She walked with Jonathan and her father past the guardhouse and out through the gate. As they made their way to the bus stop, she finally felt she was back in Germany. Observatory Hill was a world of it own, but here—out in the neighborhood—everything seemed familiar again. Red brick houses. Tidy front gardens. And the sparkle of windows that always looked just-washed.

They got off the bus at the last stop. The busy center of town was closed to cars. Shoppers filled a long, wide street lined with small shops and cafes. Jonathan bounded about like a puppy on a morning walk. He ran into every bakery, stood in the middle of the floor, and sniffed the air with his eyes closed. Elizabeth could understand why. Nothing on earth was better than a bakery in Germany. The aroma of fresh bread mingled with the smell of fancy cakes and fruit tarts and— Elizabeth spotted her favorite—cherry squares topped with buttery streusel crumbs.

The three had lunch on a bench in front of a department store. The town center was like a carnival, thought Elizabeth, or maybe a street fair. Farmers sold juicy black cherries just picked that morning. A man in a white coat held up a miracle cleaning liquid that would take out every kind of stain. And music came dancing from all directions. A flute player entertained on one side of the street. On the other side, an organ grinder cranked out music as a little monkey held out his hat for money.

By the time they were ready to head home, they had been to three different shops, filling their canvas bags with groceries. Jonathan walked slowly, balancing a cone-shaped bag of cherries in one hand and a parcel of cakes from the bakery in the other. They stepped onto a bus crowded with shoppers loaded down like themselves.

Mr. Pollack pressed a yellow signal button as the bus turned onto a shady street a few blocks down from the observatories. They paused to let an elderly lady get off first, then stopped on the sidewalk to rearrange their bags.

"Young man!" A low voice called out to them just as they reached the corner. A short, plump figure stepped out from behind a tall hedge. Elizabeth recognized the lady who had just gotten off the bus. She must have been waiting for them.

As Jonathan looked up at the old woman, his packages tilted dangerously and three black cherries plopped onto the sidewalk. On the bus they had seen her only from the back. But now she hovered before them, her round face as pale as the moon. Her white hair was pulled back tight. And her eyebrows—Elizabeth tried not to stare, but the thick black eyebrows had been painted on the woman's face. They stretched across her forehead like two dark gashes.

"Do you hear that airplane, young man?" She spoke to Mr. Pollack in slow, stiff English with a heavy German accent. "Whenever I am hearing an airplane, I am again six years old. I am with my father in an air balloon over Hamburg. I have a birthday, and I wear my best dress."

"Yes, well ... that's nice," said Mr. Pollack. The old woman took his arm and walked alongside him. "I have studied English many years ago. On the bus I heard you speak. You are American?"

"That's right. We're staying in the guesthouse on Observatory Hill. Just for a few weeks."

"Ah, yes. The observatories." She lowered her voice. "I know things about the observatories. Strange things."

Elizabeth leaned forward, waiting, but the woman began pointing to the sky again. "Do you hear that airplane, young man? Whenever I am hearing an airplane, I am again six years old, and ... "

"Excuse me," interrupted Elizabeth, "you said you know about the observatories. Have you ever heard of an astronomer named Professor Vollrath?"

"And his missing notes?" added Jonathan.

"Missing notes?" The woman turned around, as if she had just noticed Elizabeth and Jonathan. "I have heard of them. Yes. Of course." She waved her hand in the direction of the observatories. "They never will find them. My father used to say that. *They are ordinary people with ordinary minds*, he would say. *And they look in all the wrong places.*"

She stopped and put one hand on Elizabeth's shoulder. "Why do you ask about these notes?"

"We thought ... well, maybe we could try to find them," said Elizabeth. She backed up a step and freed herself from the woman's grip.

"Then you listen to what an old woman tells you. You see, I knew Professor Vollrath when I was a child. He used to be telling me ghost stories." She looked up and down the street then narrowed her eyes. "And now he himself is a ghost. He comes back to the Meridian at night to seek his telescope. Oh, yes. He knows they took it away. Every night he is coming to see if it is back." Her black eyebrows plunged down fiercely. "He comes in the night. I have seen him."

Turning around slowly, she shuffled past Mr. Pollack and began walking up the sidewalk. "It was a white dress," she muttered. "On my sixth birthday ..."

"But did your father know anything about where the notes were hidden?" called Elizabeth after her.

Too late. The woman had disappeared through a tall wooden gate. Elizabeth looked through the hedge and caught a glimpse of a small red brick house and an untidy tangle of garden. She would like to talk to the woman again. But not in there.

Elizabeth caught up with the others. "This could be important, Jon. Maybe her father knew something about where the notes are hidden. And maybe she knows too. Someone needs to talk to her again." Elizabeth pictured the two black eyebrows screaming across the old woman's forehead. "You know, I think Peter should do a test of courage, too. And I know exactly what it's going to be."

Jonathan gave a thumbs up and spilled two more cherries.

"Wow! That was quite a story!" laughed Mr. Pollack. He leaned over to Jonathan with an evil laugh. "Professor Vollrath comes at night! Bewaaaaare of the daaaaaark!" Elizabeth could see Jonathan take a hard swallow. He made a brave attempt at a smile, but he didn't laugh. Neither did she.

They waited until after dinner to tell their parents of the midnight test of courage. Elizabeth expected an immediate and firm *no*. She almost wished it. Mrs. Pollack was doubtful, but Mr. Pollack pleaded their case.

"Come on, Amanda. Let them have their little adventure. Look, Observatory Hill is fenced all around. There's a guard at the gatehouse. The scientists are out and about at night, so they won't be alone. And Professor Vollrath will keep an eye on them." He gave them a wink.

"Well … I guess," said Mrs. Pollack. "I'll stay by the window in our bedroom. If you need us, you can just shout and we'll come."

Elizabeth looked at her watch. Midnight was still two hours away. She sat on her bed and read the magazine Peter's mother had given her at the library. The short article about Professor Vollrath didn't help much with the investigation. The scientist had lived alone and never married. Besides being a well-known astronomer, he played the violin and piano. He helped start the museum at the castle and raised money for a children's hospital in Hamburg. Elizabeth took a few notes, then added one more item to her Plan of Investigation.

5. See if the old woman from the bus has any more information

She looked at her watch again, then picked up a mystery novel.

In the middle of chapter twelve, a paper airplane hit the back of her head. "Hey, Elizabeth. It's time to go."

Elizabeth closed her book, trying to ignore the fear swirling in her stomach. Her travel clock showed two minutes before midnight. "Okay. Let's get it over with. I'll tell Mom and Dad we're going."

Elizabeth and Jonathan closed the door to the apartment and hurried down the stairs. They crossed the street and stood on the steps of the Administration Building. All was quiet except for a low mechanical hum coming from one of the distant observatories.

Elizabeth looked around slowly, trying to find something familiar and comforting. But the darkness had changed everything. The wide lawns were oceans of shadow, the trees gloomy giants. Elizabeth didn't dare look at the path where they were headed.

"I don't believe in ghosts." Jonathan edged closer to his sister.

"Me neither. And I don't think old Professor Vollrath is going to be wandering around tonight." Elizabeth zipped up her jacket all the way to the top, then glanced up at the guesthouse. She couldn't see anything in the darkened windows. But her mother was there. She hoped.

From the distant castle tower, the first chime of midnight whispered through the night. Jonathan and Elizabeth didn't speak, but turned on their flashlights and moved forward. They set off on a path marked by low footlights. Just past the Big Refractor, the path curved sharply to the left and went slightly downhill. Elizabeth turned around. She could no longer see the guesthouse, hidden behind a dark line of trees.

"This is where we turn, Jon." They stopped at a point where a new path angled off to the right. It was more narrow. And dark. No need for footlights here. No one went to the old observatory at night.

Except … the flash of memory struck before Elizabeth could stop it. She thought about their first night on Observatory Hill, and the dark figure she had seen walking along the bushes.

For a few moments she and Jonathan stood in silence. The light from their flashlights stabbed weakly into the darkness. Elizabeth felt as if her body would turn to stone if she didn't move quickly. She took a deep breath, then reached for Jonathan's hand. She hadn't held hands with her brother for years. Jonathan didn't pull away.

The two made their way slowly down the path. The trees crowded close on either side now. Strange. Elizabeth couldn't feel even a whisper of wind, yet the long branches rustled and swayed as if … she tried not to think of it … as if the trees were moving on their own.

Soon the rough feel of weeds underfoot told Elizabeth they were near the abandoned observatory. Then … a sudden rustling in the bushes. Elizabeth could feel Jonathan's fear jolt from his hand to hers. They backed up a few steps then relaxed as a fat hedgehog waddled across the path in front of them. Elizabeth took a few steps forward then swung her flashlight upwards. She could see the curve of a metal roof. The Meridian Observatory was just ahead, its dark bulk hidden in the night. They had nearly reached their goal. The stairway where Peter had placed the stone was only a few yards away.

Elizabeth stood stiff as a statue, shivering slightly in the damp air. To reach the stairs they would have to step off the path and cross the dark strip of grass that lay in between. Her legs refused. What was it about the night that turned the world upside down, and made walking three steps seem like the hardest thing in the world? Elizabeth's thoughts slid away to another place. Another night. She could see herself at her grandfather's lake house. She was standing under the stars on a narrow pier as the black water slapped against the wood. Leaving the safety of the path would be like stepping into that dark deep water.

She could feel Jonathan pulling away. She knew he wanted to turn around and go back.

"We have to get the stone, Jon. We can't come this far and not get it." She led Jonathan off the path, staying as far away from the bushes as possible. Finally they reached the bottom of the steps.

"There it is!" Jonathan trained the beam of his flashlight on the top step. Elizabeth let go of his hand as she hurried up the steps and grabbed the stone. She turned around to give a triumphant smile.

"We did it, Jon. Now ... " Her next word was buried in an avalanche of sound. Elizabeth raised her arms, as if to protect herself from the screech of metal on metal that tore through the darkness. Wild with terror, she took four stairs in one leap and landed next to Jonathan. She knew in an instant what was happening. The roof of the abandoned observatory ... was opening!

CHAPTER 5

INVESTIGATING THE SCENE

"Stay together!" Elizabeth reached out in the darkness and managed to catch the sleeve of her brother's jacket. Jonathan took off like a bolting horse. They ran, half stumbling, down the path toward the guesthouse. Elizabeth didn't dare look back at the old observatory. Her mind didn't believe in ghosts, but her legs were sure Professor Vollrath's pale skeleton fingers reached out just inches behind her.

They took one wrong turn and had to cut across the soccer field. Elizabeth could see the beam of Jonathan's flashlight bouncing wildly on the dark grass. Finally they were back on the lighted path and within sight of the guesthouse. As they dashed past the steps of the Big Refractor, an astronomer had to step out of the way to avoid a collision.

The two burst up the stairs of the guesthouse and found their parents waiting at the top.

"The roof!" shouted Jonathan. "It started to open!"

"Not so loud. The lady downstairs is sleeping." Mrs. Pollack hustled them through the door and into the kitchen. Elizabeth threw herself into a chair to keep her knees from shaking.

"What are you talking about?" asked Mrs. Pollack. "What roof?"

"Didn't you hear that sound?" Elizabeth spoke in a fierce whisper. "There's someone inside the old observatory making the roof open up."

Mr. Pollack's eyebrows started their dance of doubt. "But there's no telescope in there. There hasn't been for years."

"I know," said Jonathan. "That's why we have to call the police. Or go wake up Karl or something."

"Now let's just wait a minute." Mr. Pollack put his hands on Jonathan's shoulders. "We need to talk about this before we start waking people up. I did hear something, but it sounded more like … a train putting on the brakes."

"Are you sure the roof was opening?" asked Mrs. Pollack. "Did you actually see it?"

"No, but we heard it," insisted Elizabeth. "And the stairs were shaking. It wasn't a train, I know it wasn't." She looked down at her hand. Her fingers, still stiff from fear, clutched the telescope rock. But her flashlight was gone.

"And I dropped my flashlight," she said miserably. "I guess it must be on the path somewhere."

Mrs. Pollack took the flashlight from Jonathan. "All right. Your father and I are going to find out what's going on before we do anything else. We'll look around for your flashlight, too."

Jonathan grabbed his father's hand. "You're going to leave us here alone?"

"Don't worry. We'll be right back. Lock the door and watch from the window."

Elizabeth and Jonathan turned off the light in the bedroom and peeked out from between the heavy brown curtains. Their parents hurried down the lighted path past the Big Refractor. Elizabeth watched as their bodies blurred into shadow. The last thing she could see were her mother's bright white sneakers, marching down the path as if they had a life of their own. And then, nothing but darkness.

Elizabeth had never felt so far away from Indiana. "Please, hurry," she whispered. Jonathan didn't say a word. The two stood at the window, not daring to move. A few minutes later, the beams of

44

two flashlights bobbed along the path. The dark shadows took their familiar shapes.

Jonathan and Elizabeth ran to the door. "What did you see?" called Elizabeth.

Mr. Pollack stepped softly up the stairs. "I'm not sure if you'll be relieved or disappointed, but the roof of the Meridian Observatory is shut tight. The door is locked. There's no sign of anything strange there."

"But ... " Elizabeth shook her head.

"It's not hard to explain," said Mrs. Pollack. "You heard the screeching of train wheels nearby and just assumed it was the roof opening up. You were all alone by a spooky old building at midnight. It's easy to see why your imagination took over."

"Maybe," mumbled Elizabeth. Every time her parents didn't believe something, they started talking about her imagination. But the sound of metal grating against metal. And the steps vibrating under her feet. How could that have been a faraway train?

"Well, at least we found your flashlight," said Mr. Pollack. "It was at the bottom of the steps."

Jonathan ran into the kitchen. "The signal! We forgot to signal Peter." Elizabeth followed him through the kitchen to the back balcony. Jonathan shined his flashlight on his watch. "I'll tell you when to start and stop," he said. "We have the telescope rock, so we're supposed to do ten seconds of short blinks."

Elizabeth turned in the direction of Peter's house and blinked rapidly into the darkness until Jonathan told her to stop. As soon as she stopped, her signal was answered by four blinks.

"He got the message," said Elizabeth. "And now we have to signal a meeting. Let's tell him to meet us at ten." Elizabeth made a slow circle with her flashlight, then blinked ten times. Another four blinks from Peter.

By the time Elizabeth flopped into bed, Jonathan was already sleeping. Elizabeth's mind was muddled. Why would someone open up the roof of the old observatory? Was someone trying to scare them? But only her parents and Peter knew they were going to the Meridian Observatory at midnight. Maybe the sound *was* just a faraway train. And maybe tomorrow—in the daylight—everything would be more clear.

"Jon, come on. Finish your breakfast." Elizabeth had long ago given up trying to understand her brother. What kind of kid would read *The Encyclopedia of the Totally Disgusting* while eating breakfast?

"Tapeworms are really neat," announced Jonathan. "They can live in your intestines. Then they keep growing and growing until they're really long. One time a doctor pulled out a tapeworm. And it was forty feet long. So he put it in a jar of alcohol and kept it." Jonathan took an enthusiastic bite of bread and jam. "Wanna see a picture? It's a close-up."

Elizabeth gave him her best wilting stare. "Just finish your breakfast. We have to go."

Peter was already in the lean-to when Jonathan and Elizabeth ducked through the doorway.

"Our proof of courage," said Elizabeth. She laid the telescope rock in the middle of the dirt floor.

Peter nodded in approval. "You are now official members of the Star Detective Club."

"You mean the *Three* Star Detective Club," said Elizabeth.

"Well … okay." Peter gave each a solemn handshake. "But what happened last night? You took so long to signal."

"I'll tell you," said Elizabeth. "But first I need to know something. Are there any railroad tracks near here?"

"Some old tracks at the bottom of the hill, but they're not used anymore."

"Not used anymore?" Elizabeth felt an icy stab of fear.

"We went to the Meridian," began Jonathan, "at midnight. Just like we said we would. Elizabeth picked up the stone and then we heard this weird scraping noise."

"I heard something too," said Peter. "What was it?"

"I'll tell you what it was," said Elizabeth, "but I don't know if you'll believe it." She took a deep breath. "The roof of the old observatory started opening up. I was standing right on the steps."

Peter opened his mouth, but nothing came out.

"And the whole stairway started shaking. I dropped my flashlight, and we ran back to the guesthouse. Then my mom and dad walked over to get my flashlight. But the roof was closed. Like nothing had happened."

"So they don't believe the roof opened," added Jonathan. "They think it was just a train putting on the brakes."

"Oh, man." Peter stood up. He was glowing like a 200-watt bulb. "This is the best thing that's ever happened." He pointed importantly with his finger. "Number one. Investigate the scene of the crime. Then we'll talk to Karl. I'm sure he'll believe us."

Peter scrambled out the door and took off down the path. "I'll meet you at the observatory," he called over his shoulder. "I have to get my equipment. Don't do anything until I get there."

"Equipment?" Elizabeth rolled her eyes. She and Jonathan ran out of the woods and cut across the soccer field. At the edge of the tall grass, they hesitated. Last night's fear seemed to be waiting for them, hanging in the air like a mist. The dim drizzle that began to fall didn't help.

"Let's go, Jon." Elizabeth hurried through the wet grass. As she cut through the line of bushes onto the overgrown path, she felt the gloom of the place close in on her.

Elizabeth made herself walk briskly. When she reached the observatory, she pointed to the edge of the bottom stair. "That cigarette butt wasn't there yesterday, Jon. I know it wasn't." Elizabeth thought about the picture of Professor Vollrath. And the cigarette dangling from his fingers.

"Don't touch the evidence!" Peter came pounding down the path. He wore a long white laboratory coat and carried a bulky black suitcase. A cell phone and two small tools dangled from his belt.

Setting the suitcase on the stairs, Peter snapped it open. Jonathan's jaw nearly dropped to his shoes when he saw the display of detective equipment. Tweezers, medicine droppers, evidence bags, pieces of chalk, latex gloves, ruler and measuring tape, magnifying glass, brushes, small containers of liquid and powders. On the inside of the lid, straps held a set of tools in place.

"Stand aside." Peter pulled a small digital camera out of his pocket. He took a few close-ups of the cigarette butt next to the stairs, then pulled out a pair of tweezers. Carefully he picked up the evidence and dropped it into a plastic bag. "This," he announced, "is going to give us a lot of information."

Elizabeth looked at it doubtfully. She had never paid any attention to cigarette butts. In fact, she hardly knew anyone who smoked. But Peter, as usual, was an expert.

He held up the bag and studied it with a magnifying glass. "Number one. It's a Sonnengold Extra cigarette. I can tell by the gold band on the tip. Not one of the most popular brands. Number two. There's no lipstick, so the smoker must be a man."

"Or a woman who doesn't wear lipstick," said Elizabeth.

"Oh … right. And third, whoever it is, he's really hooked. It's smoked all the way down to the filter. There's no tobacco left at all." Peter looked up as if he expected applause.

"Maybe it's just Karl's cigarette," said Elizabeth. "He's the caretaker. He could have been here this morning."

"Karl doesn't smoke. And no one else would have a reason to come here."

Peter dropped the evidence bag into his detective case and pulled out a small bottle. He nudged past Elizabeth and walked up the stairs to the metal door. After sprinkling black powder on the door handle, he gently brushed the powder across the metal. "I don't see any fingerprints. Only smudges." Peter stood up and dusted a spot of powder off his white lab coat.

"Well, if it isn't Dr. Peter Hoffmann," said a deep voice. "Looks like you're ready to take out someone's appendix."

Peter jumped down the stairs. "Karl! You're just the person we wanted to see! Someone was here last night."

"Here?"

"Inside the observatory. And the roof started opening up."

"That's impossible," laughed Karl. "There's only one key to the building. When I go home it's locked in the director's office." He pulled out a bundle of keys. "It's right here. And there's no telescope inside. The roof hasn't been opened for years."

"But we felt it," said Elizabeth. "Jonathan and I were here last night. At midnight. I heard the noise and felt the stairs shaking."

"You two were here at midnight? Alone?" Karl's smile faded. "That explains the complaint I had this morning. One of our astronomers said he was almost run down by two children late last night." He turned to Peter. "And I suppose this has something to do with you."

"Of course," said Peter. "I gave them a test of courage. So they could get into my detective club. They had to come to the observatory alone at midnight. That's when the roof started opening up."

"But a few minutes later it was closed," added Jonathan, "so my mom and dad think we just imagined it."

"Well, I'll have to agree with your parents. Why would anyone want to be in the observatory? There's nothing in there but some old furniture." He walked up the stairs and slowly ran his hand over the door. "No sign that the door was forced open."

Karl turned around. "I'll have someone look into this, but ... " he looked at them intently, "I want you to promise not to wander around here after dark. This is a scientific community, and it's not your playground." He looked at Peter's open detective case. "I don't know what kind of game you kids are playing, but I just hope you don't go too far."

Elizabeth looked down at the steps in silence. She had planned to ask Karl to take them into the observatory to search for the missing notes, but now she couldn't. Not with Karl so displeased. With one more stern look at Peter, he turned away and marched down the path.

"I'm beginning to think we did imagine this," said Elizabeth softly.

"Then you're not a very good Sherlock Holmes," said Jonathan. "Because he would know we didn't make it up." Jonathan looked up at the door and crossed his arms. "It's elementary."

Elizabeth curled her lip at her brother. He was showing off for Peter, she was sure.

"Look up there." Jonathan pointed to the door. Elizabeth glanced at the door handle, then groaned. How could she have missed it? The spider was gone. Only a few silky strands hung from the door frame. Someone had disturbed the web to get into the observatory. Someone who was sneaking around at night.

"Good work, Jon. Somebody brushed the spider away after we were here yesterday afternoon. And there's something else." Elizabeth thought about their very first night on Observatory Hill. "The first night we were here I looked out the window around midnight. I saw someone by the bushes near the entrance gate. There was this little flash of light, like the person was lighting a cigarette. Then the shadow moved along the bushes ... toward the old observatory."

Peter snapped his case shut. "Let's go look. We might find some more evidence."

The three made their way back to the entrance gate across from the guesthouse, then walked along the line of tall bushes toward the Meridian Observatory. Elizabeth saw some people staring at them. She wished Peter would take off his lab coat.

"Spread out," he ordered. "Walk along the bushes, one arm's length apart. And don't take your eyes off the ground. If the person lit a cigarette, we should be able to find it." After a few minutes of walking along the hedge, Elizabeth noticed the stand of trees became thicker. They were near the old observatory.

"Halt!" Peter stopped and pointed to the grass. Elizabeth didn't know whether she felt like a detective or like a dog being trained. Peter opened his detective case again. He knelt down, took another picture, then carefully tweezed a small piece of white from the grass. "This must be it. The cigarette the person lit when you were looking out the window." He dropped it into the plastic bag. "It's a Sonnengold Extra. The same as the other cigarette we found."

"So if it's the same kind of cigarette," said Elizabeth, "that might mean the person who was here last night was here two nights ago too. And maybe ... "

Peter smiled. "Maybe whoever it is will come back again tonight. And this time," he added, "we're going to be ready!" He rooted around in his black case and held up a small bottle of bright purple liquid. "Introducing The Peter Hoffmann Super Sleuth Foolproof Intruder Trap ... Extraordinaire."

CHAPTER 6

A LONG NIGHT

Elizabeth stared at the bottle. Why did she always have the feeling Peter was going to get them into trouble? "So what's in there?"

Peter was already running toward the old observatory. "Staining liquid," he yelled.

"Cool!" Jonathan sprinted after him.

By the time Elizabeth caught up with them, Peter and Jonathan were standing by the metal door of the Meridian Observatory. Peter held the bottle in one hand and a small brush in the other. "I just paint this on the door handle," he said. "So whoever opens the door is going to have a purple hand for a few days. The stain can't be washed off!" Peter grinned triumphantly. Jonathan's joy sent him running in circles around the nearest tree. "Purple hand," he chanted. "He'll have a purple hand." Elizabeth looked at the two boys. Jonathan … multiplied by Peter. She had a sinking feeling her life was never going to be the same.

She ran up the stairs. "Peter, wait! What if Karl opens the door today and gets his hand purple? I mean, he's already kind of mad at us."

"Oh … right." Peter put the cap back on the bottle. "Don't worry. Karl goes home around seven o'clock. I won't brush it on until after he leaves. And if it's smeared tomorrow morning, it will prove to him and all the other grown-ups that someone was here. If not, I'll just wipe it off."

"Well, I still don't think it's a good idea."

"Don't worry. I know what I'm doing." Peter closed his detective case. "But I have to go now. I need to put these pictures into the computer and type up my findings. We'll meet here again this afternoon at three. And try to think of some more ideas. We need to be ready for our visitor tonight." He took off at a slow trot, his white lab coat flapping behind him.

After lunch, Elizabeth sat cross-legged on the bed, bent over her detective notebook. She turned to an empty page and stared at the blank lines. She had to think of a good idea for tonight. Something that would impress Peter and prove to the grown-ups someone was coming to the old observatory.

Elizabeth shifted her shoulders as she felt a tickle on her back, then at the top of her ear. And then in her ponytail. Elizabeth reached back, ready to swat a fly. Instead, she found herself shaking hands with a set of bony fingers. She jerked her hand away and scrambled off the bed. Waving in the air was a plastic skeleton hand. Attached to a broom handle. Attached—of course—to Jonathan.

Elizabeth gave a tug and pulled her brother into the room. "Don't you have anything better to do? Like finding out who's sneaking into the old observatory. We're supposed to be real detectives, you know. We'd better come up with something."

"I don't know. I'll think about it later. First I want to use this back scratcher on Dad."

Elizabeth picked up her notebook again. *Ideas for tonight*, she wrote. She tapped her pen on the page, underlined the words twice, then put a box around them. She couldn't think of a thing. Her mind began to wander. She wrote *old mystery* on one side of the page, and underneath, three dots in the shape of a triangle. Where did Professor Vollrath hide his notes so long ago? She wrote *new mystery* on the other side. And who is sneaking into the old observatory where he used to work? Suddenly Elizabeth thought about the strange fortune cookie the man at the airport had given her. *The dim haze of mystery brings old and new together.* Elizabeth drew a line between *old mystery* and *new mystery.* What if they were connected? Maybe someone was trying to scare them off so they would stop looking for the notes? But why would anyone care if they found the notes? Elizabeth scratched out the line and tore the page out of her notebook.

"Looks to me like you're stuck on something." Her father walked into the room. "Jon and I are going to the castle. Why don't you come along? I think you need to freshen up your brain cells."

Elizabeth closed her notebook. Maybe her dad was right. Her brain cells felt about as lively as a glass of flat soda pop.

The three left through the main gate and walked around the corner. A shady path ran along the outside of the wrought-iron fence enclosing the observatories. On one side of the path the white domes of the observatories peeked through the trees. On the other, the hillside fell steeply. Far below stretched a storybook world of thatched-roof farmhouses and long, narrow fields.

"Now I know where we are," said Elizabeth. "This is the corner where the Meridian Observatory is, and the path to the castle starts right here."

As soon as they turned toward the castle, Elizabeth could feel herself slipping into a world of long ago. Ancient trees, standing straight as soldiers, towered on both sides of the path. The moss-covered branches gave the air an eerie shimmer of green. Just ahead, the red-brick castle rose up like a mighty ship, strong and stern against the iron sky. It wasn't hard to imagine the past here. Lords and ladies. Knights and kings and queens.

The end of the path opened to a large garden, glowing with sweet-scented roses. Tourists and townspeople strolled on the crisscross paths and rested on benches. Elizabeth took a picture of her father by a flaming red climbing rose.

"Take me! Take a picture! Quick." Jonathan stood next to a small bridge leading over the moat to the castle. Elizabeth took a picture, managing to include a swan gliding past on the dark green water.

"Did you get it in the picture?" asked Jonathan.

"Yeah, I got the swan."

"Not the swan! The *rat*." Jonathan pointed under the bridge to the edge of the moat. Elizabeth could see a pair of fat gray haunches and a snaky tail disappear into the tall grass. "I bet they have lots more inside. Probably in the dungeon." Jonathan ran across the bridge into the cobblestone courtyard of the castle.

Elizabeth made her way slowly across the uneven stones and looked up at a set of giant-sized wooden doors. A hand-lettered sign announced that the museum was closed for renovations until September. She and Jonathan peeked into one of the windows and could see a room cluttered with swords and suits of armor. Jonathan thought he spotted a torture instrument, but it turned out to be a crowbar. Two workers used it to pry open a large wooden crate.

"I'm gonna go look for that rat again. Maybe I can find the hole." Jonathan took off toward the bridge. By the time Elizabeth and her father reached the moat, he was nowhere in sight. Mr. Pollack called him twice but there was no answer. Elizabeth felt a knot of fear. Too many unexpected things were happening. And now Jonathan had vanished into thin air in a matter of seconds. Mr. Pollack called louder.

"Over here! But I don't know how to get out." Jonathan's muffled voice seemed to come from behind a high hedge which ran along the side of the garden. But how did he get there? Elizabeth and her father walked along the hedge until they came to a small opening. They stepped through and found themselves on a narrow gravel path with high bushes on either side. They turned left at first, and ended up at a dead end. They retraced their steps and turned right, but after two turns they were at a dead end again. "I feel like I'm lost in a maze." Elizabeth turned around. "Dad?" Great. Now her father was gone too. Elizabeth tried to retrace her steps, but couldn't remember if she had come from the right or the left. And even on tiptoe she couldn't see over the bushes.

"Dad!" She called louder this time. Mr. Pollack peeked through an opening in the bushes. "No wonder Jonathan got lost," he said. "This is a garden maze." He cupped his hands and yelled. "Stay where you are, Jon. We'll come and get you." They started again at the beginning. "The paths are laid out just like a maze on paper," said Mr. Pollack. "If this is a simple branching maze, all we have to do is reach out with one hand and walk with that hand always touching the bushes. It's not the shortest way, but it will get you to the center and out again." They soon found their way to the center, where a small fountain bubbled softly. But still no Jonathan.

"Jonathan?" Elizabeth was half afraid and half angry. "Where are you?"

"I'm on the other side," came a voice. "By the wall."

Elizabeth and her father wound their way to the other side of the maze and came out at the outer wall of the castle. They found Jonathan on a patch of grass between rows of bright red and yellow flowers. He was on his knees, calmly investigating a mole hill. "No more disappearing," said Mr. Pollack. "Just stay with us." Elizabeth was ready to hurry back, but Mr. Pollack insisted on taking the last picture. She and Jonathan stood in front of an arched wooden door set into the castle wall.

"I thought of an idea," whispered Jonathan. "For tonight." Elizabeth didn't say anything. Her brain might be refreshed, but that didn't help a bit. She dreaded telling Peter the Great she had no ideas.

By the time they reached the guesthouse, it was almost time to meet Peter.

Jonathan ran up to the apartment and came out with a small plastic bucket and shovel. "I'm gonna set a trap," he said. "What's your idea?"

"It's … well … I'm still thinking." Elizabeth looked at the front of the house. High up, near the peak of the roof, a small half circle of window looked out like an open eye. Suddenly, she had her idea.

Peter was already sitting on the steps of the Meridian Observatory. He had his black case with him, but at least he wasn't wearing the white lab coat.

"Okay," he said, "I'm ready for your ideas." Elizabeth let Jonathan go first. His idea was clever, she had to admit. Digging around with his shovel, he made four mounds of sand. The grass was full of mole hills, and Jonathan's looked exactly like the others.

"It's a footprint trap," he announced. "If someone goes up the stairs, he'll step on it and leave a footprint in the sand."

Peter patted Jonathan on the back. "You're a genius, my boy." He turned to Elizabeth. "So what's your idea?"

"Follow me." Elizabeth led the boys down the winding path back to the guesthouse. She took them up the stairs to the door of their apartment, then turned to face a second door.

"I think this is the door to the attic." She pressed down the handle, but the door was locked. "We need to get the key from the lady who takes care of the house. And keep it until tomorrow morning." She looked at Peter. If there was persuading to do, he was the one to do it.

"Leave it to me," said Peter. "Frau Schultz is a friend of mine. I've known her all my life."

Elizabeth and Jonathan sat on the stairs. They watched Peter knock on the downstairs door and disappear into the apartment. He returned ten minutes later, shaking his head. "That wasn't easy. She said we could go up in the attic, but we're not supposed to snoop around and touch things."

He unlocked the door with a long, old-fashioned key. The three made their way up a narrow staircase. At the top Peter used another key to open a second door. They stepped into a large dim room under a pointed roof. Elizabeth loved the hot, dusty smell of a good attic. And this one was just right—a bare-bones place of rough old wood and shadowy corners. She didn't see much that would tempt them to snoop, though, only an old vacuum cleaner and a few folding chairs.

"This is my idea," she said. "Over here." They ducked under a set of towels and shirts hanging on a clothesline between the beams. Elizabeth led them to the far wall, where a small window looked out over Observatory Hill. The view was just as she had hoped. They could see the entrance gate and most of the path to the Meridian Observatory.

"Jon and I can take turns keeping watch tonight. We won't be breaking our promise to Karl, because we won't be outside."

Jonathan pressed his face against the glass. "But I can't see very much. Everything's so far away."

"Technology," said Peter. He snapped open his suitcase and produced a small pair of binoculars. "Ultra compact. Automatic focus. High magnification."

When Elizabeth looked through the eye pieces, she felt like taking a step back. The binoculars reached out to the world and brought it right up to her face. She could look through the windows of the Administration Building and see papers lying on desks. She could see Professor Bergstrom walking by and could even read the name of the bookstore on the bag he carried.

"These are perfect. So as soon as it gets dark, Jon and I will start watching. Probably about ten o'clock. We'll stay as long as we can."

"And I'll brush the staining liquid on the door handle after Karl leaves," said Peter. "We'll meet tomorrow morning. Ten thirty at the lean-to. Then we'll go collect the evidence."

It was just before dark when Elizabeth and Jonathan tiptoed up the attic stairs. Their parents had agreed to let them go, but Elizabeth could tell they were tired of getting strange requests.

"I'll take the first shift, Jon. Then we'll switch every fifteen minutes. You can use your flashlight to read a book, but keep the light away from the window."

Elizabeth pulled a wooden folding chair up to the window. She stared out, keeping her eyes on the entrance gate. A ray of moonlight struggled through the clouds. In the dim glow she saw the guard lock the gate and leave for the night.

"Hey, Elizabeth. I wouldn't want to get near your oxter." Elizabeth rolled her eyes but said nothing. Jonathan continued. "And your hallux isn't too pretty either. Your pollex would probably be okay, unless it had a bleb on it or maybe a hairy nevus."

Elizabeth shook her head. She was definitely slipping. She had forgotten to hide *The Encyclopedia of the Totally Disgusting.* "Jonathan, quit babbling."

"I'm not babbling. They're real words. There's a whole list in my book. *Oxter* means armpit, which is why I wouldn't want to be anywhere near *your* oxter. And *hallux* is the big toe. *Pollex* means thumb, and *bleb* is a blister. And a *hairy nevus* is … Here, I'll show you a picture. It's a … "

"Jonathan, if you don't stop, I'll flush that thing down the toilet."

Jonathan quieted down, except for an occasional snicker.

By the time Elizabeth was on her fourth shift, she decided that keeping watch wasn't her favorite part of detective work. Staring into the darkness at nothing in particular had to be the most boring job in the world. She looked at her watch. Eleven thirty.

Elizabeth crossed her arms tightly. She was beginning to feel chilly. And something about the dark, lonely attic made her feel homesick for Indiana, too. She closed her eyes and pictured her room at home. Everything was so clear. She could see the posters on the wall, the sun streaming in through the big double window, the white curtains floating on a breeze. Then she was outside in the garden. Watching the sunflowers. Strange. They kept growing. And growing. And suddenly the sunflowers were as tall as the trees.

When she opened her eyes, Elizabeth found that her head was leaning against the wall. She sat up straight in the chair and rubbed her stiff neck. As she clicked on her flashlight and glanced at her watch, she winced. Ten minutes before midnight. She had been sleeping for twenty minutes. Why didn't Jonathan wake her up? She shined her flashlight on her brother. He was stretched out, peacefully sleeping with his head resting on *The Encyclopedia of the Totally Disgusting*.

Elizabeth put down the flashlight and looked out the window. Everything looked the same, empty and still, but who knows what she had missed? She moved the chair closer to the window, determined not to shut her eyes for a second. Suddenly she put her ear to the window. The dull throb of a motor broke through the stillness, coming nearer. Elizabeth glanced over to the entrance gate.

A few seconds later, everything began happening fast. So fast she had no time to awaken Jonathan. A car glided slowly up to the gate. The headlights blinked twice. It seemed to be some kind of signal, because a man wearing a light-colored jacket suddenly stepped out of the shadows. He hurried past the guesthouse and toward the entrance. Looking over his shoulder, he unlocked a small door in the gate. As he did so, a figure in dark clothing slipped out of the car and came through the opening.

Elizabeth's hands were shaking so hard, she could barely grip the binoculars. The dark figure threw something down on the ground. The two talked for a moment, then cut across the grass to the tall hedge. One thing was certain. They were headed in the direction of the Meridian Observatory.

Elizabeth almost wished the binoculars weren't so powerful. She was safe in the attic, she told herself, high up and far away, but the binoculars made the figures seem close. Too close.

Elizabeth watched as they walked along the hedge. Suddenly the man in the light jacket turned around and looked up at the guesthouse. For one terrifying instant the face seemed to be looking straight at her. Elizabeth nearly dropped the binoculars as she jumped off the chair and scurried away from the window. She pressed her back against the wall. It couldn't be. It was impossible. But ... the man looking up at the house was Karl!

CHAPTER 7

TROUBLE!

Elizabeth stood with her palms against the wall and her eyes squeezed shut. Maybe closing her eyes would undo what she had just seen. How could it be true? Karl sneaking around at night, taking someone to the old observatory! She thought about this morning. When they told Karl someone had been at the Meridian Observatory, he didn't even believe them. Or was he just pretending?

When Elizabeth opened her eyes she saw the flashlight glowing on the floor. She had forgotten to turn it off. What if the two men had seen the faint light in the attic window? Pushing away from the wall, she forced herself to move. First she crawled over to the flashlight and turned it off. Then, her hands still trembling, she knelt in front of the window and looked through the binoculars again. This time the men were nowhere to be seen. The car was gone. Nothing stirred on Observatory Hill. As if a book had been shut and the story was over.

Elizabeth turned away from the window. The room was all darkness and shadow, except for the white shirts on the clothesline. They hung upside down, with long, limp arms, as if they were hovering in midair. Suddenly Elizabeth wanted to get out. She shook Jonathan awake and led him, mumbling and protesting, down the attic stairs. He shuffled into the apartment like a zombie and rolled onto his bed.

Elizabeth stuck her head into the kitchen doorway. Her parents sat at the table in a small circle of light. Mrs. Pollack was writing and Mr. Pollack read the newspaper. Watching them made Elizabeth feel safe again, like being warmed by a cozy fire.

Mr. Pollack looked up and smiled. "So. Any mysterious midnight happenings?"

"Well … kind of. But I'll tell you about it later." Tomorrow, thought Elizabeth. Tomorrow she would smooth out her tangled-up thoughts.

The next morning, before Jonathan was awake, Elizabeth sat up in bed and opened her detective notebook. She wrote down everything she could remember about the strange midnight scene. The words took up only three lines. She had no description of the car, and she couldn't say much about the person who got out of the car. But one fact was sure—it was Karl's face she had seen in the moonlight.

"Hey! How did I get here?" Jonathan emerged from the covers looking like his hair had been whipped up with an egg beater. He groped around under his pillow. "And where's my *Encyclopedia of the Totally Disgusting?*" Elizabeth smiled. The book had been left in the attic. And with any luck at all, a pack of rats might have eaten it during the night. But Jonathan had already taken the key from the night table. She could hear his footsteps pounding up the stairs and hurrying across the floor overhead.

Jonathan had no time to read during breakfast. Elizabeth told him about the mysterious figures who appeared at midnight. She decided not to tell him about Karl. Not yet.

As they hurried down the wooded path, they could see Peter pacing up and down in his white lab coat. All three ducked into the small opening of the lean-to. Elizabeth and Jonathan squeezed together on a log next to Peter's detective case.

She handed Peter the binoculars. "Something happened last night." Elizabeth described the scene. The signal with the headlights. The man opening the gate. Then the two sneaking along the bushes toward the Meridian Observatory.

"You saw the criminals?" Peter rubbed his hands together.

"Perfect. What's the description?"

"Well, the one who got out of the car—I think it was a man. And he had a dark jacket on. That's all I could see. But the other man. I … I saw his face. Through the binoculars."

Peter leaned forward. "And?"

Elizabeth felt like she was chewing on sawdust. "The man who opened the gate was Karl," she said softly.

Peter jumped up and hit his head on the board at the top of the lean-to. "*Absoluter Quatsch[2].*" His German poured out so fast Elizabeth could barely understand. "It couldn't have been Karl. I've known him all my life. He wouldn't lie to us. Or pretend he didn't know about someone coming to the observatory." Peter sat down again. "You said you fell asleep. You were tired, and you made a mistake."

"But I … "

Peter shook his head. "Karl has nothing to do with this."

Elizabeth sat silently. Peter could think what he wanted, but he was breaking the most important rule for detectives. A good detective follows the evidence wherever it goes, even if that place is uncomfortable or unexpected.

"What about the car?" asked Jonathan.

"And the license number?" added Peter. "Did you get the license number?"

Elizabeth felt a flush of heat rising in her cheeks. "Everything happened so fast. I had to keep watching the two people, so I couldn't look at the car. It was a dark color. Or maybe light. I don't know. Maybe both."

Peter stood up and buttoned up his white lab coat. "Let's forget about the car for now. It's time to gather evidence." He grabbed his suitcase and ducked out the low opening. "On to the scene of the crime."

Jonathan trotted after him. "First we have to go by the gate. Elizabeth said the man who got out of the car threw something down."

Elizabeth took her time walking down the wooded path. She

---

[2]Absoluter Quatsch (Aab-zo-looter Kvoch)! Absolutely ridiculous!

refused to run after Peter like a dog following its master.

She could see the other two ahead of her. Peter walked briskly, waving to everyone he passed.

"How's the mystery going? Any luck figuring out the three dots?" Elizabeth spun around and saw Professor Bergstrom coming down the steps of the Big Refractor Observatory.

"Oh ... well, I ... I haven't had much time. But I did go to the library and look at the exhibit. And sometime I want to look inside the Meridian Observatory. We think maybe he hid the notes in there."

"Why don't you ask Karl if you can look around? I'm sure he would let you in. We can try to find him now, if you'd like."

"Karl? Now?" Elizabeth took a step back. Karl was the last person she wanted to see. "Uh, that's okay. I have to go find my brother." Elizabeth hurried away and headed toward the front gate. By the time she caught up with the boys, they had already reached the main entrance. The wide metal gate was open and a guard sat in the tiny gatehouse.

"This is where I saw them," she whispered. "They talked for a minute, and then the man who came from the car threw something down." Elizabeth scanned the grass while Peter walked in a slow circle. Jonathan, as usual, had found a stick and was poking around in the bushes.

"Over here!" He squatted down in front of a pudgy bush with small yellow flowers. As he held back a branch, Elizabeth could see a speck of white on the ground underneath. Peter snapped open his detective case. He took out a tweezers and held up a cigarette butt. "Sonnengold Extra," he announced. "Smoked right down to the filter."

"So the man who came last night was the same one as before," said Elizabeth. "He keeps coming back at midnight. Again and again."

As Peter dropped the cigarette into the evidence bag, the guard stepped out of the gatehouse. When he saw Peter he gave a friendly wave, then stood for moment staring at the detective case. Elizabeth hoped the man wasn't going to ask any questions.

"I wanna see if my footprint trap worked." Jonathan jogged down the curved path that led to the abandoned observatory. Three 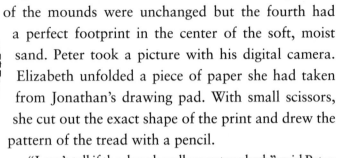 of the mounds were unchanged but the fourth had a perfect footprint in the center of the soft, moist sand. Peter took a picture with his digital camera. Elizabeth unfolded a piece of paper she had taken from Jonathan's drawing pad. With small scissors, she cut out the exact shape of the print and drew the pattern of the tread with a pencil.

"I can't tell if the door handle was touched," said Peter. He took a special rag from his detective case and wiped the staining liquid off the door. "We'll just have to be on the lookout for someone with a purple hand." He leaned over the footprint. "But we can find out what kind of shoe this is. There's a big shoe store in town. We can take the bus there."

"By ourselves?" asked Jonathan. "I don't think Mom will let us."

Peter strode off swinging his detective case. "Don't worry. It's easy. Child's play. I take the city bus to school every day. Your mom just needs to be convinced."

"Yeah. Peter the Great," muttered Elizabeth.

A few minutes later Elizabeth had to admit she was impressed. Peter could have been a professional persuader, if there were such a thing. He rolled out his arguments, one, two, three, as if his idea was the most logical thing in the world. He soon had their parents convinced to let them go into town by themselves.

"Cell phone," said Peter, patting his pocket. "Call me anytime when you want to check on us." He handed Mr. Pollack a slip of paper with his phone number on it.

They got off the bus in the center of town. Elizabeth had promised to keep an eye on Jonathan. She was ready to catch him by the collar if he started wandering, but he stayed close. She didn't even have to drag him out of any bakeries. They soon reached the busy pedestrian street, still bustling with shoppers. The organ grinder was there with his monkey again, but the man in the white coat was selling a miracle vegetable chopper instead of stain remover.

After a stop at Peter's favorite food stand, they settled onto a bench, each holding a fat roll with a long sausage sticking out on either side. Elizabeth sat up as straight as she could. Being in town on their own made her feel tall, somehow. And very grown-up.

"So where's that shoe place?" Elizabeth stood up as soon as she was finished—before Peter could start giving orders. The three made their way down the crowded street, leaving a cluster of pigeons strutting after their bread crumbs.

The Shoe Palace was one big, brightly lit room, a maze of shoe racks filled from top to bottom. Behind the counter stood the only employee, a young woman with red lips and bottle-black hair. Elizabeth unfolded her drawing of the footprint and handed it to Peter. "This is the pattern we need to match," she whispered. "So we need to look at the sole of every single shoe." The three went to the men's section and split up. Elizabeth worked her way through two shelves of shoes, turning over each sneaker to inspect the bottom. She could see the saleslady put on a pair of black-framed glasses and peer at them.

Suddenly the young woman stepped out from behind the counter and made her way directly toward Elizabeth. In a panic, Elizabeth slipped over to the ladies' section and grabbed a shoe. She bent down as if she were going to try it on. She looked up and gave a wilted smile. It was a skinny high-heeled shoe in bright red leather, ridiculously big for her.

She was saved by Peter, who was making a commotion at the other side of the store. "I found it!" he yelled. As several customers looked on, he waved a shoe in the air.

Jonathan and Elizabeth rushed over to Peter. He held the shoe up against the paper. "A perfect fit. Our stranger is a very tall man. Jaguar sneakers. Size forty-eight."

Jonathan began the Outer Mongolian Warrior Dance, racing around a display of men's sandals. "Forty-eight!" he shouted. "Size forty-eight! He's a giant!"

"Forty-eight is the *German* size, Jon, not the American." She caught him by the arm. "And quit yelling. You're going to get us in trouble."

Peter walked to the counter to smooth things over with the saleslady. Elizabeth could hear bits and pieces of his explanation. Detectives. Working on a very important case. Would probably be in the newspaper some day. The young woman nodded, looking slightly baffled.

Elizabeth sighed. A very important case. But what case? Some man was coming to the abandoned observatory at midnight every night. They knew what kind of cigarettes he smoked and what kind of shoes he wore. But their so-called case was just a jumble of details that didn't fit together. This wasn't like the other mysteries they had solved. Something strange was going on, and Karl was involved. She knew it was time to talk to the grown-ups.

In front of the train station, an army of shoppers got onto the bus. Leafy green vegetables, fresh flowers, and fruit peeked out from baskets and bags. Elizabeth stood in the back of the bus, wedged in between a stroller and a large man with two bags of groceries. Feeling something wet on the back of her hand, she turned to see the copper-colored snout of a tiny dachshund. The dog sat in a canvas bag on a woman's lap. Elizabeth smiled and tried to find a more comfortable spot. She had never seen a bus so crowded. Everyone was squeezed in shoulder to shoulder except ... She stretched to the right and could see Jonathan and Peter standing near the back door. They stood in complete comfort, with Cheshire-cat smiles and at least three feet of room on either side.

Elizabeth stood on her toes and leaned over. On the floor by their feet was some kind of disgusting splat. It looked like ... Elizabeth squinted

... Jonathan's rubber vomit. Size extra large. The other passengers had stepped back, leaning away from the mess. Just before getting off the bus, Jonathan reached down and calmly picked it up. Elizabeth heard one woman gasp.

"Jonathan, you are just too weird." On the way back to the observatories, Elizabeth walked behind the boys. She peeked into the overgrown garden of the old woman who had told the ghostly story about Professor Vollrath. They had never found out if the strange woman with the painted eyebrows had more information about the missing notes. Elizabeth made a plan. As soon as they figured out what was going on at the Meridian Observatory, she and Jonathan would get back to the case of Professor Vollrath.

Elizabeth barely noticed the police car parked on the street. As they reached the gate of the observatory grounds, though, she turned around and looked at the green and white car. The word *Polizei* was written on the side, just like the helicopter she had seen when they were talking to Professor Bergstrom. Elizabeth couldn't stop staring at the police car. An uneasy tingle crept up her arms.

"You know, Peter, I ..." But Peter and Jonathan had already walked through the gate. Just then the guard stepped out of the gatehouse. Peter gave him a smile, but this time the guard didn't smile back. "You are to go home immediately, Peter." He turned and faced the others. "*Alle drei.*" All three. Something about his voice—dry and sharp—made Elizabeth feel like she was about to be sentenced to ten years hard labor.

She walked through the gate, feeling her stomach go into a tailspin. She wasn't sure why, but she knew one thing for sure. Elizabeth and Jonathan Pollack, ace detectives, were in big trouble.

CHAPTER 8

THE MYSTERIOUS STRANGER

Peter walked down the sidewalk past the guesthouse. "I think he meant we're all supposed to go to my house." If Peter was worried, he didn't show it. He strolled along, bestowing his royal wave on a few scientists coming down the steps of the Big Refractor Observatory.

Elizabeth didn't wave to anyone. She forced herself forward, feeling like she was walking through molasses on a pair of wooden legs. Even Jonathan had lost his bounce. He followed close behind, meek as a baby deer.

Peter's family lived on the second floor of a white stucco building behind the guesthouse. Peter took the outside steps two at a time and unlocked a heavy wooden door. He led the way up a stairway and motioned them into a square hallway inside the apartment. Elizabeth may have felt grown-up walking around in town, but here the high ceilings and large white doors made her feel small. And now, behind one of the doors, their doom awaited. Her mouth turned desert dry at the thought.

"They're probably in here." Peter pushed open a wide door leading to an airy living room lined with bookcases. Elizabeth almost felt as if she had walked back outside. A row of long windows brought the green summer day into the room. On the sills, flowering plants crowded brightly against the glass.

The pleasant room brought little comfort, for it was full of people, and they didn't look a bit happy. Mr. and Mrs. Pollack sat stiffly on a long brown couch. Two other adults sat in straight-backed chairs across from them. Elizabeth recognized Peter's mother and assumed the husky man next to her was his father.

She pulled Jonathan into the room by the sleeve of his jacket. In front of the windows stood a tall young man, a stranger. Elizabeth glanced up nervously, noticing his short blond hair, neatly trimmed beard, and ... his hand. The palm of his right hand glared like a neon sign—unmistakably purple! Elizabeth looked at Jonathan and Peter. The midnight intruder stood before them.

Peter's father stood up. "Peter, there's someone here who would like to talk to the three of you. This is Inspector Heinz Fischer ... of the Hamburg Police."

The police? Elizabeth's legs turned from wood to jelly. Now she knew why seeing the police car parked on the street had made her uneasy. The car that had signaled with its lights at midnight. She remembered now. Its color was dark *and* light—the green and white color of a police car. She slipped onto the couch in the corner and made room for Jonathan.

Peter walked up to the policeman and shook the man's purple hand, wishing him a good day. *"Guten Tag, Inspektor Fischer.* The Three Star Detective Club already knows a lot about you. You've come to the Meridian Observatory at midnight for at least three days. You wear Jaguar sneakers, size forty-eight, and you smoke Sonnengold Extra cigarettes, always right down to the filter. You should really stop smoking, you know." Peter slid into a deep chair, his arms slung over the sides. Elizabeth noticed his hands quivering.

"Peter!" said his mother sharply. "I think you had better listen to what Inspector Fischer has to say, instead of telling him what size shoe he wears."

"I have something important to tell you," said Inspector Fischer slowly. He looked serious, but not unfriendly. "I know that the three of you have been …" he looked down at his purple hand, "playing detective, but this time it's not just a game. You've stumbled onto something that is very secret and must remain so. I can't give you much information, but I can tell you that the police are using the old observatory as an observation point. We have several other look-outs in the area. It's part of a major investigation."

"So that's why you opened up the roof of the observatory?" asked Peter. "You were going to look out the top?"

"Oh … that." Inspector Fischer edged his mouth into a weak smile. "I had been there a few days before, just to look around. But that was my first night inside the observatory. Actually, I was trying to put on the light. I stupidly pressed the wrong button. No one was more surprised than I was when the roof began to open. I had hoped no one would notice my mistake, but Karl told me that two of you had been there. And then we saw someone spying through the attic window last night."

Elizabeth bent down and slowly retied each of her shoes.

"It is very important that this operation remain secret," continued the inspector. "I must ask you to tell no one about this matter. Only Karl and the director of Observatory Hill know about this. And most important, I must warn you not to wander around at night—not here and not on the castle grounds. Do you understand?"

All three nodded their heads solemnly. The policeman shook hands with the adults and turned to leave. "By the way," he said, turning to Peter, "how did you know my shoe size?"

Peter explained how they had each come up with an idea about investigating the midnight stranger. Inspector Fischer smiled when he heard that Jonathan had set up mounds of sand to look like mole hills.

"You three have made things … well … complicated for me," he said. "But I must praise your detective work. I'll leave my card here. If you see anything suspicious during your investigations, your *daytime* investigations, that is, let me know." He handed the card to Peter. "And please," he added as he held up his purple hand, "no more staining liquid."

After the policeman left, the grown-ups sat in silence for a moment. It reminded Elizabeth of the quiet seconds between a flash of lightning and a roar of thunder. She knew a lecture was coming. Mr. Pollack turned toward Elizabeth and Jonathan. He spoke in German, so Peter and his parents would understand. "I don't know what's going on here. I thought you were trying to find Professor Vollrath's notes. And now you're mixed up in a police investigation."

"We *were* working on the missing notes," said Elizabeth. "But then those strange things started happening at the observatory. All we wanted to do was get some evidence, so we could prove to you that someone was sneaking into the observatory at night. We didn't mean to get in trouble."

"And the idea about the staining liquid was mine," added Peter. "Elizabeth tried to talk me out of it."

Each parent took a turn, and by the end of four stern lectures, they had promised four times to follow Inspector Fischer's instructions. Once the lectures were over, Peter's father walked out of the room. Soon, a comfortable smell of brewing coffee officially changed the subject. After Peter's mother set down a plate piled with cookies, the parents began to talk about other things. Boring grown-up talk, but for Elizabeth, it was as sweet as a lullaby. She relaxed, sinking back against the thick cushions of the couch. Finally, no one was talking about messing up a police investigation.

A police investigation. Elizabeth's mind wrapped itself around the words and wouldn't let go. A major investigation, the policeman had said. Right here under their noses. But what were the police investigating? The mystery of the midnight intruder was solved, but it

73

had only led to another, bigger mystery.

Elizabeth looked up at the sound of a low hiss. Peter stood by the door, motioning for them to follow. Jonathan swooped down on the cookies one more time, taking one for each hand and two for his pockets. No one seemed to notice as the three walked out.

"I'll show you my room," said Peter. "I mean, my detective laboratory." He led them back into the hallway. "I have everything," he said with a wave of his hand. "Everything."

Before Elizabeth could roll her eyes, Peter opened another wide door off the hallway.

Jonathan stood in the doorway, speechless, and even Elizabeth's jaw dropped an inch or two. She felt as if she had just entered Command Central of the local police department. A long white table stood in the middle of the room. At one end of the table the detective case was open, displaying its wares. But that was just the beginning. The table was cluttered with equipment from one end to the other. Computer. Printer. Two microscopes. Vials of powders and beakers full of liquid. Thick, hardcover books. The walls were papered with newspaper articles about local crimes, and above Peter's narrow bed hung a map of Hamburg, stuck with colored pins.

Elizabeth sighed. Her entire set of detective equipment consisted of a well-worn copy of *How to Think Like a Detective*, a magnifying glass, a flashlight, and a red spiral notebook. It didn't even fill up a small backpack.

Peter stood in the middle of the room. "So what do you think?"

"Well ... I guess you do have everything," said Elizabeth.

"I think it's awesome." Jonathan plopped down on a wheeled desk chair and began spinning around. With two cookies stuffed in his mouth, he scooted the chair across the wooden floor, narrowly missing Elizabeth's toe.

Elizabeth glared at her brother. Sherlock Holmes was lucky. *His* trusty assistant was a doctor, not a chocolate-covered kid brother who walked around with rubber vomit in his pocket. "Jon, you're never going to be a detective if you can't sit still for one second. We need to think about things. Like what case Inspector Fischer is working on."

"Yeah? Well, maybe I'm the best detective here." Jonathan licked a blob of chocolate off his thumb, then wiped his hands on his pants. "I already know what case Inspector Fischer is working on."

"You do *not* know what case he's working on."

"I do too. He's right there." Jonathan pointed up at a picture in the middle of a newspaper clipping taped to the wall. The picture showed a large house with a police car in front. Next to the car was a policeman at least a head taller than his partner.

Elizabeth gave a doubtful huff, but took a closer look at the picture anyway. Jonathan was right. She recognized Inspector Fischer's short hair and neat goatee. "I don't get it, Jon. How do you notice things like that?" Jonathan reminded her of the steel ball in a pinball machine. He kept bouncing around and occasionally hit the jackpot.

Peter clapped Jonathan on the back. "Excellent work, my man! Now we know what he's working on. That picture goes with the article about the villa burglaries."

Elizabeth looked up at the picture. "The what?"

"The villa burglaries. There's a lake in Hamburg called the Alster," said Peter, "with lots of fancy mansions around it. Someone has been breaking into the houses and stealing silver and jewelry. Small stuff easy to carry off." Peter walked over to his wall map and pointed to a lake edged with five red push pins. "I marked all the locations. It's been going on for months." He sat down at his computer and clicked open a file. "I know all about the case. The burglaries happen every ten to fifteen days. The last one was a week ago."

"But it doesn't make sense," said Elizabeth. "The castle is nowhere near the villas. So what does it have to do with the break-ins?"

Jonathan rolled his chair back across the room. "Maybe the police think the thieves are going to steal something from the castle."

"I don't think so," said Peter. "They've been fixing up the castle for a long time. They moved all the valuable things out."

Elizabeth pictured the castle, looming dark and lonely at the top of the hill. Why would a gang of thieves want to hang around a castle at night? Unless … "Wait a minute. What if the police think the gang is using the castle to hide the things they stole? You know, until things cool down and they can sell them."

"Exactly!" Now it was Elizabeth's turn to receive a hefty clap on the back. "So all we have to do," Peter continued, "is find out where the loot is hidden. I can see the headlines now—*Peter Hoffmann Solves Case That Eluded Police.*"

"What?" Elizabeth stood with her hands on her hips.

"Oh … sorry. *Peter Hoffmann and Friends Solve Case That Eluded Police.*"

"Except I don't think we're supposed to be working on the case," said Jonathan. "We're already in trouble."

Peter tapped the business card in his shirt pocket. "But Inspector Fischer told us we should report anything suspicious. We could look around the castle in the daytime."

"I have an idea," said Elizabeth. "Let's give it one try. Tomorrow we'll go to the castle park. If we don't find any evidence, we'll forget this case and just work on finding Professor Vollrath's notes."

Peter and Jonathan nodded their heads. The next day would either be the beginning—or the end—of their investigation into the villa burglaries.

CHAPTER 9

ANOTHER TRAP

Elizabeth had just finished her last spoonful of cereal when Peter's whistle sounded from below. "Uh, Mom. Peter and Jon and I were thinking about going to the castle this morning. You know, just to look around."

Mrs. Pollack tilted her head to the left, the way she always did when she was about to say no. "I don't like the idea of you kids snooping around the castle. I don't know what the police are investigating, but there must be something going on around there."

"But, Mom, it's not dangerous. The park is always full of people. And we'll all be together. Besides, we won't be snooping." Elizabeth glanced out the window. "Peter doesn't even have his detective case. Or his white lab coat."

"I'll give you one hour," said Mrs. Pollack. "I want you back before I leave for the University."

Elizabeth and Jonathan clattered down the stairs and found Peter slouched on a bench across from the guesthouse. His head hung low, and even his spikes of hair seemed to droop. "I'm ruined," he moaned. "Ruined. My parents won't let me take my detective case outside. For the rest of the summer. So how are we supposed to investigate?"

"Don't worry," said Elizabeth. "We just have to … think. You know. Use our brain power." She ignored Jonathan, who was grinning at her with a mega wad of green chewing gum stuck to his front teeth. "Of course, *some* of us might have the brain power of a tsetse fly."

"Tsetse fly," shouted Jonathan. "I'm a tsetse fly." He stretched out his arms and began running around the nearest tree.

Elizabeth grabbed her brother before he could work himself up to the Outer Mongolian Warrior Dance. "Come on. We have to get going. Mom says we only have an hour."

Peter snapped out of his slump. "Follow me. I know a shortcut." He led them across the soccer field and past the farthest observatory. When he reached a locked metal gate, he put his foot on the handle and quickly hoisted himself over. Elizabeth and Jonathan did the same, then followed Peter down a shady gravel path. They came to a sharp curve and then … the castle. Elizabeth stopped, almost startled by the strong red brick against the blue sky. Suddenly a cloud sped across the sun. For a moment, the towers and turrets plunged into shadow, then flickered back to sunlight. Elizabeth had a strange feeling, as if the castle had winked its eye and invited her to explore its secrets. She ran full speed to catch up with Peter and Jonathan.

At the rose garden, the three stopped to catch their breath. Elizabeth stepped into the sun. The warmth felt good, just enough to soften the morning chill.

"What are we supposed to do now?" asked Jonathan.

"We look for traces," said Elizabeth. "*How to Think Like a Detective,* chapter four." She hooked Jonathan's arm so he couldn't run away. "My detective manual says everything that happens leaves traces behind. It's just that most people don't see them. That's the difference between detectives and ordinary people. If the robbers are hiding things around here, there must be some way to tell. We just have to be smart enough to find the traces."

"Well, I don't know about traces," said Peter. "But I'm going to look for suspicious characters. I know exactly how to do it without being noticed. Just leave it to me."

"Peter the Great will show you the way," mumbled Elizabeth. She and Jonathan watched while Peter walked among the mothers pushing strollers and the tourists admiring the flowers.

Peter cupped his hands behind his back, strolling slowly along the square path framing the garden. He looked up at the clouds, bent down to examine the flowers, and tied his shoes several times. All the while he gave everybody a good looking-over. Elizabeth didn't see anyone who seemed the least bit like a jewel thief. A dark-haired man in a suit sat on a bench reading the newspaper while his young daughter played nearby. On the next bench, an unshaven man holding a half-filled bottle had a lively conversation with himself.

Tying his shoe for the third time, Peter bent down next to two gray-haired ladies. They sat huddled in conversation, with their heads nearly touching. Peter leaned over and peered into their canvas shopping bags, as if he expected to see a diamond necklace sticking out.

Suddenly one of the ladies grabbed her bag and clutched it to her chest. The other shook her finger at Peter. Elizabeth couldn't hear everything she said. Something about young people today and no manners.

Peter trotted back to Jonathan and Elizabeth. "It's all clear. Nothing interesting, except ... " He leaned closer. "Except him." Without turning around, Peter jerked his head in the direction of the man with the bottle. "Undercover agent. In disguise. He's a policeman keeping an eye on the castle. I'm sure of it."

Elizabeth glanced over at the man. His eyes were closed now, and he was snoring lightly. "How do you know?"

"I could tell he had something in his pocket." Peter whispered behind his hand. "Probably a cell phone."

Or another bottle, thought Elizabeth. "Right. Anyway, let's look around in the courtyard. We don't have much time." The three hurried toward the bridge that arched over the narrow moat. As they walked past the unshaven man, Peter leaned over and spoke into his ear. "We're working on the same case, brother." The man's eyes popped open. He gave Peter a sloppy smile and offered him a swig from his bottle.

After crossing the bridge, they made their way over the uneven cobblestones. The courtyard bustled with workers carrying tools and buckets of paint. Elizabeth noticed that the windows were covered by heavy iron grates, and the main door had a sturdy lock.

"I don't see how anyone could get in here at night," she said. "Besides, it wouldn't be a good place to hide anything. Too many people."

"I found something!" Jonathan was back on the bridge, bent over the railing. Elizabeth and Peter hurried over. "Look over there." He pointed toward the long grass at the edge of the moat. "It's the rat hole. I saw him again."

"Jonathan, can't you keep your mind on the mystery? We're supposed to be looking for ... I don't know. Something suspicious."

Elizabeth looked up from the bridge. She could see the other side of the castle now. The upper windows were too high to climb into and the lower ones were covered by grates, just like the ones in the courtyard.

She wandered back toward the garden, drawn by the sweet smell of the roses. The sun was strong now, and the garden hummed with bees. Elizabeth watched an artist set up his easel under the broad limbs of a tree. Why, she thought, would anyone want to hide jewels in such a busy place? A park full of people. Workers all over. Maybe the castle didn't have any secrets after all.

"Hey, hello!" Peter rushed past Elizabeth, waving with both arms in the direction of the garden. His wave was answered by a young man trimming a rose bush. "That's Henning Biermann," he called to Elizabeth. "He's a friend of mine."

"I know. You've known him all your life."

"Exactly." Peter ran over to his friend.

Elizabeth sat down on a bench on the sunny side of the garden. So much for the Three Star Detective Club. One star was gabbing with his friend. Another star couldn't think about anything except rats. And the third star was out of ideas.

"I'm going in the maze," shouted Jonathan. "It's really cool in there." He clomped across the bridge and ran toward the small opening in the hedge.

"Jon, we don't have much time left. We'll get lost in there."

Peter came running over. "No, we won't. I know the maze like the back of my hand. It's child's play. Just leave it to me." Peter led the way, trotting confidently through the maze until they came to the bubbling fountain at the center. They continued to the other side and came out of the maze at the castle. Elizabeth recognized the old wooden door and the bright flowers hugging the brick wall.

"This is where we were yesterday. With Dad."

"Hey, I can beat you to the fountain." Jonathan took off at a run, with Peter following. They raced through the opening in the hedge and disappeared into the maze.

"Wait a minute!" Elizabeth hurried down the path after them. She didn't want to be left behind, but ... she stopped suddenly and turned around. The flowers. Something about the flowers wasn't right. She walked back to the castle wall, then knelt down on the stepping stones in front of the old wooden door. The flowers by the door were the kind she knew from home. Lemon-yellow marigolds and frilly petunias. But the size. That was it. The plants near the door were the same kind as the others in the garden, but smaller. Elizabeth leaned in farther and felt the ground around the plants. The dirt felt loose. She smiled to herself, feeling as if she should be wearing a cape and a Sherlock Holmes hat. Now she knew why the plants looked different. Someone had been digging around in the garden and put in new flowers on both sides of the door. Next to the path she could see the wilted stem from one of the old plants.

Elizabeth got up and walked along the wall. None of the other flowers were newly planted.

"Hey, Elizabeth. Watch out. I think you have a hairy nevus on your oxter." Elizabeth stiffened. She didn't have to turn around to know that Mr. *Encyclopedia of the Totally Disgusting* was standing behind her.

"Jonathan, I meant what I said about flushing that thing down the toilet." She spun around and faced the two boys.

"How come you're still here?" asked Peter. "Jonathan and I have been through the maze twice."

"I'm still here because I'm investigating. And I figured out something." Elizabeth walked back to the door. "Someone," she announced, "took out the flowers that were here and planted new ones."

Peter shrugged. "The flowers probably had some kind of plant disease. So they put new ones in."

"Or maybe," added Jonathan, "they had a hairy nevus on their …"

"Jonathan?" Elizabeth narrowed her eyes and made a flushing motion with her hand.

"Okay. Uh … maybe bugs ate them."

"But all the other flowers in the garden look healthy. Why would bugs just eat the ones by the door?" Elizabeth shook her head. "We have to know more about the flowers. Data. That's what Sherlock Holmes would say. We need more data."

"And I know where to get it. Wait here." Peter crunched down the gravel path and disappeared into the maze. He trotted back a few minutes later. "I just talked to Henning, the man who was working in the garden. He told me this door is never used. It leads down to the dungeon." Jonathan hopped in a circle at this good news. "No one goes down there because they've never fixed up that part of the castle. And he said they've had a good summer. They planted these flowers in May, and they haven't had to plant any new ones."

"Haven't had to plant any new flowers?" Elizabeth felt like she was speeding downhill on a roller coaster. Her ideas rushed so fast she could barely keep up with them. "So that means somebody else planted these flowers." She paced up and down in front of the door. "The robbers could be coming here at night. And using the dungeon to hide the things they stole. But when they came through the door, some of the plants got crushed, so they had to plant new ones. That way no one would get suspicious about the dead flowers. And then no one would … Jonathan, you're not even listening."

Jonathan wagged his tongue back and forth, balancing his chewing gum on the tip. "I am too. And I think what you're saying is weird."

"Well, you *would* think it's weird, 'cause you're so weird yourself." She looked at Peter.

"I don't know," he said. "Using the dungeon to hide things? But look at the door. It looks like it hasn't been opened in a hundred years."

Elizabeth tiptoed over the stepping stones leading to the door. Heavy strips of rusty metal were bolted to the wood, holding the cracked and dry timbers together. The door had no handle, only an enormous keyhole that gave a glimpse of the gloom within. Elizabeth ran her hand along the ancient wood. "But what if we could prove the door has been opened."

Peter's his eyes lit up. "If I just had my detective case, we could use my electronic sensor and then … "

"Forget it," said Elizabeth. "No more high tech. What we really need is ... " She stared at her brother. "Jonathan, spit out your gum."

"Huh?"

"Your gum. Spit it out in your hand."

Jonathan grinned. Leaning over, he plopped a glistening green heap into his open hand. He bowed as he held it up to Elizabeth's face.

"Dinner is served, my lady."

Elizabeth pasted on a smile. "Thank you, Jonathan. This is just what we need."

"Need for what?" asked Peter.

"Elementary, my dear Watson." Elizabeth ignored Jonathan's grimace. "With this little lad's simple piece of chewing gum, the Three Star Detective Club is going to catch the villa gang." She let the words hang in the air for a moment. "Child's play," she said. "Just leave it to me."

Elizabeth stretched out her ponytail and plucked out a long brown hair. "All I do is hold the hair across the door where it opens. And Jonathan, you put half the gum on each end to hold it. That's right. Perfect." Elizabeth straightened up. "And now just put some dirt on the gum, so it'll be the same color as the door."

"I get it," said Peter. "The hair is stretched across the door, so when it opens the hair breaks in two."

"Exactly. And when that happens, we go to Inspector Fischer."

"How come we can't tell the police to look in the dungeon right now?" asked Jonathan.

"Because if we're wrong, then we'll really look stupid. We don't want to bother the police unless we're sure. Otherwise—" Elizabeth turned her head slightly. "Move away from the door. And don't turn around." In the opening to the maze she had seen two gray heads peeking out of the bushes.

"Those two ladies are watching us," she whispered. "The ones who got mad when you looked in their bags. They probably think we're doing something to the castle."

Peter stepped back and made a sweeping motion with his arm. "And to finish our tour," he shouted, "observe the unusual, uh, the unusual ... wood on the door to the dungeon. And the unusual ... brick on the castle wall. Some of the bricks are laid out the long way, and some have the short end in front. They're laid out long, short, long, short. It's called Flemish bond."

"Thank you," shouted Elizabeth, "for your interesting tour." The two gray heads slipped back behind the bushes.

"How did you know about that?" asked Elizabeth.

"I used to come here on field trips with my school." Peter looked around and spoke in a low voice. "I can check the door every morning. Henning said I can come and help him with the garden work. And get paid."

"So the next time the villa gang breaks in somewhere," said Elizabeth, "they'll come here to put the stuff in the dungeon. And the hair will be broken the next morning. All we have to do is wait." She glanced at the hedge, where she thought she could see a pair of eyes behind the leaves. "And hope we don't get into trouble."

CHAPTER 10

PETER'S PROOF OF COURAGE

Elizabeth awoke to find a giant gray-green eye hovering over her face. She squeezed her eyes shut, then opened them again. The eye was still there, peering at her through a magnifying glass. She didn't have to put her glasses on to know who it was. "Jonathan, you're crazy. Get away from me!"

"I'm just checking out your eyelashes." Jonathan moved the magnifying glass back and forth. The giant eye squinted. "I think I see one. My *Encyclopedia* says bacteria live all over your body. Millions. Billions. Zillions. And mites and fungi, too." Elizabeth groaned. THE BOOK. Of course. She put her pillow over her head, but she could still hear.

"Face mites are the best. You can see them under a microscope, and they look like little tadpoles with stumpy legs in front. They can live in your pores or on your eyelashes. They dive right down into the hair ..."

Elizabeth threw the pillow at Jonathan as she shot out of bed and into the kitchen.

"It's called ..." Jonathan stopped running and sounded out the words. "*De-mo-dex fol-lic-u-lo-rum*. You gotta see the picture." Jonathan rushed at his sister, holding the open book. "It's a close-up. So you can see all the little legs." After a chase that took them three times around the kitchen table, Mr. Pollack walked into the room.

"Hand over the book, Jon. You know the rule. No *Encyclopedia of the Totally Disgusting* before breakfast."

"Don't worry," called Mrs. Pollack from the hallway, "I have something that's going to get your mind off the book." She walked in, pulling a sheet of paper out of her briefcase. "I checked my e-mail at the University yesterday, and I printed out a message for you. Sorry, I forgot to give it to you last night."

Jonathan put down his book. "Who's it from?"

"I'll let you guess. The message starts, *How do you work this blasted thing, anyway?*"

"Pop!" Two voices shouted the word at the same time. Pop was Elizabeth and Jonathan's grandfather. He was a grumbly eighty-two year old, whose hobbies were reading the dictionary and giving advice to everyone around him.

"But how can Pop have e-mail?" asked Jonathan. "He hates computers."

"Uncle Rudy gave him a computer. Kind of a thank-you gift for helping with the case of the ancient coins last spring. I wrote to him about your new case—that you're trying to find some missing scientific notes." She set the note on the table.

Elizabeth and Jonathan read the message together.

Subject: New Case—missing scientific notes

From: Pop

To: The Detectives

How do you work this blasted thing, anyway? I'm
not sure this will get to you, but Hello, Elizabeth and
Jonathan. This is your old grandpappy here, typing

with two fingers. I'm going to give you some advice about your new mystery, so pay attention. Why don't people find things? Because they assume something is true, but it's not. That's called making a false assumption. One time I was looking for a book, and I was sure it had a blue cover. I looked everywhere but couldn't find it. Then it turned out my memory was wrong. I thought the cover was blue, but it wasn't. That was my false assumption. The book really had a red cover, and that's why I wasn't finding it. If those scientific notes haven't been found for eighty years, someone is making a false assumption. Find that false assumption, and you'll have a chance.

Elizabeth thought about the missing notes. She didn't know what kind of false assumption they could be making. Everyone knows what scientific notes look like. They would be numbers written on the pages of a book, just like the one in the display case.

Elizabeth slid the message into her detective notebook. She had almost forgotten about Professor Vollrath's missing notes. Her mind had been on the villa robberies and nothing else. They had been waiting for three days now.

Peter kept an eye on the castle. For two hours each morning he helped out in the garden. The man with the bottle—Peter still insisted he was an undercover agent—was there every day. And so were the gray-haired ladies. The two watched Peter like a hawk, but he managed to slip away and check the door every day. Nothing happened. The hair wasn't broken, and there had been no more villa burglaries.

"Hey, asparagus legs!"

Elizabeth swatted away the skeleton hand that patted her shoulder.

"I know. We're supposed to go and meet Peter." They raced into the woods and saw Peter jogging down the path from the other direction. One by one they crawled through the small opening of the lean-to. As usual, Peter reported that the door hadn't been disturbed. The man with the bottle wasn't there this time, but the two ladies were.

"And just before I left," said Peter. "They told me they're going to report us to the director of the museum. For vandalizing the castle."

"Report us? To the museum director?" Elizabeth coughed, trying to block the panic rising in her throat. Jonathan hiccupped. They had already gotten in trouble with the police, and now the director of the castle museum. Elizabeth studied Peter's face. She didn't understand him. Disaster was about to strike, and he sat there as contented as a cow.

"Peter, do you ... get in trouble a lot?"

"All the time. That's why everyone knows me. My mother says I suffer from over-enthusiasm. My father says I just don't think. But it's okay. They're used to it. And I never do anything wrong on purpose."

Elizabeth opened her spiral detective notebook. "Well, maybe we should get back to our other case. Try to find the missing notes. At least we're not in trouble about that." She looked at her plan of investigation. "We still need to search the Meridian Observatory. So we have to convince Karl to let us in." Elizabeth and Jonathan looked at Peter.

"Child's play," he said. "Leave it to me. I'll talk to Karl after lunch." He ducked out through the doorway and motioned them to follow. When he raised his pointer finger, Elizabeth knew he was about to get bossy. "Okay," said Peter. "Listen carefully."

If Elizabeth hadn't been eleven years old, she would have stuck out her tongue at Peter. Instead she rolled her eyes and stared at the top of the nearest tree.

"I'll leave a message for you at the four-footed tree."

"The what?" Elizabeth looked down.

"This one." Peter pointed to a giant tree at the edge of the woods. The smooth gray bark had formed clumps at the bottom, as if the tree were standing on four over-sized clown feet.

"I'll make an x with two sticks if we can't do it today. But if Karl says we can, the sticks will tell you the time. Two sticks mean two o'clock. Half a stick is thirty minutes. So three and a half sticks would mean three thirty."

"How come you can't just ring the doorbell," asked Elizabeth, "and tell us when to meet? Or call us."

"Too easy," said Peter as he trotted away. "You're the one who says we're supposed to use our brains."

After lunch, Elizabeth studied her notes about Professor Vollrath. She felt like the old pendulum clock at her grandfather's house, going back and forth between the new mystery and the old. Today the pendulum had swung back to the old mystery. She opened the bedroom window and leaned out. Two astronomers were eating their lunch on the steps of the Big Refractor. Others walked along the paths toward the smaller observatories. Professor Vollrath's notes had been missing for more than eighty years. And all that time, scientists were living and working on Observatory Hill. Why had no one found the hidden notes?

Elizabeth saw Jonathan dart across the grass and head toward the four-footed tree. A few minutes later he stomped up the stairs. "We get to go inside the Meridian! We're supposed to be there at two and a half sticks."

At exactly two thirty, all members of the Three Star Detective Club waited on the steps of the abandoned observatory. As soon as Elizabeth spotted Karl, she ran up the path to meet him. She was determined not to let Peter start giving orders.

"We'd like to look at the stone building first," she said. "The one that looks like a little temple."

"That's fine." Karl walked up to the small building next to the Meridian Observatory. He pulled a weighty set of keys from the pocket of his coveralls. After unlocking the rusty padlock, he pushed hard with his shoulder against the wooden door. It stuck, then heaved open, unloosing a blast of damp, sour air.

"Let's take everything out." Elizabeth helped the two boys carry out two small tables and a set of folding chairs. Karl waited outside while the three crowded into the tiny square room. As soon as Elizabeth turned on her flashlight, she lost hope of finding anything. From top to bottom, the room was made of blocks of stone. Smooth, cold—and solid. By the time she finished searching the room, Peter and Jonathan were already on the steps of the observatory. Elizabeth stood in the doorway. She took one last, long look, but she knew the room had nothing to hide.

She stepped outside and took a gulp of fresh air, sweet and heavy with the smell of coming rain. They would have to hurry if they didn't want to get wet.

"How come you two never wait for me?" She ran up the steps of the old observatory as Karl swung open the metal door. The pale light from the open door quickly melted into darkness. Karl clicked on two bare bulbs that hung from the ceiling on long cords.

"I'm afraid this isn't very interesting," he said. "Just some old furniture. We use the extra chairs when we have big meetings." He pointed to the corner. "That box over there is off limits. Completely. You know Inspector Fischer has been using the observatory. He stores some of his night vision equipment in the box." Peter's eyes lit up but he promised not to touch anything.

Karl helped them move the wooden chairs to one side of the room. "I have some things to do in the tool shed. Let me know when you're done, so I can lock up." Halfway down the steps, he spun around. "And Peter …"

A chorus of three voices finished the sentence. "No more staining liquid." Karl smiled and slipped away down the path.

With the chairs out of the way, not much remained. Three battered wooden desks. Three chunky black telephones. A long scar in the linoleum floor was the only hint that a telescope had once been there.

The desks were searched inside and out. Jonathan piled up their finds on the floor—four stubby pencils and a dried-up eraser. Elizabeth stood in the middle of the room. She turned in a slow circle, sweeping her gaze over the metal walls. Three dots, she repeated to herself. Maybe the three dots are here.

Elizabeth was facing away from the door when she heard shuffling on the stairs. She whirled around.

A thin, eager face peeked in the doorway. Elizabeth didn't recognize the old woman. She was tall and willowy. And everything about her—her hair, her skin—was so pale. Like the dry color of tall grass in winter.

"Professor Bergstrom!" Peter went to the door and helped the elderly woman into the room.

Elizabeth and Jonathan looked at each other. "But I thought …"

"I'm the second Professor Bergstrom. The one you met is Olaf. My husband." She spoke with the same pleasant singsong as her husband. Leaning heavily on her cane, she eased onto a chair.

"You mean you're an astronomer, too?" asked Jonathan.

"Yes. For many years my husband and I worked at the Big Refractor. But now"—she tapped her leg with her cane—"bad knees. Such a nuisance. These old legs cannot bring me up the stairs to the telescope. So I am once again a stargazer. I look up at the stars, as I did when I was a girl in Sweden. Just for their beauty."

She motioned to the row of chairs next to her. "Come sit with me. I want to ask you how your investigation is coming. Olaf told me you're looking for the missing notes of Professor Vollrath."

"It's not going very well," said Elizabeth. "I don't know. It seems kind of silly to think we could find those notebooks when so many people have already looked for them."

The professor nodded her head slowly. "I am going to tell you something. Something I have never before told anyone. When I first came here, many, many years ago, I also tried to find the notes. I was the first woman astronomer to work here, and I thought I would show those stuffy old men how smart I was. I sneaked around like a thief in the night. Searched every building on the grounds, not once, but twice. I found nothing. And now," she laughed, "I also am a stuffy old professor."

"Did you look in Professor Vollrath's house?" asked Elizabeth.

"Oh, yes. His house was here. On the observatory grounds. I searched every inch of the house before it was torn down. I'm convinced the notes were not hidden there. No. I feel that something simple has been overlooked. And of course no one has ever understood the meaning of the three dots."

Jonathan stood up. "Pop, I mean our grandfather, thinks we're making a ... what does he think we're making?" He looked at Elizabeth.

"He says everyone is making a false assumption. So maybe we think the notes look a certain way, and that's what we're looking for. But the notes might look different. And that's why no one can find them."

"A false assumption," repeated Professor Bergstrom. "Yes. I shall think about that. But now I must go before the rain comes."

Peter carefully helped her out of the chair and down the stairs. Elizabeth watched. Maybe Peter was nicer than she thought—at least when he wasn't bragging or being bossy. But still, she would have to keep him in line.

As soon as he came back, they searched the desks once more. Then they tapped the metal walls and even used Peter's binoculars to look for three dots on the high, arched ceiling. Nothing. Elizabeth dropped onto a high-backed chair with her detective notebook on her lap. The smell of rain was stronger now, but only a few drops plopped against the metal roof. The thunder kept its distance, growling faintly. Elizabeth looked at her *Plan of Investigation*. She smiled. Gloomy day. Distant thunder. And one more thing left to do on her list.

"Peter!" She clapped him on the back. "It's time for your proof of courage."

"What? But I started the club and I don't have to . . ."

"Unless you're afraid."

"No, of course not."

"There's a house down the street with a messy old garden. And the woman who lives there has black eyebrows painted on her face."

"I know it," said Peter. "The *Hexenhaus*[3]. That's what we used to call it."

"She talked to us," said Jonathan. "And she said her father knew something about the missing notes."

"So all you have to do," added Elizabeth, "is talk her into an interview."

"An interview … with her?" Peter's eyes narrowed for a moment, as if someone had pinched him. Then he crossed his arms and leaned back in his chair. "Sure, I can do it. Child's play. We can go there right now."

"Okay," said Elizabeth. "You two go tell Karl we're done, and I'll tell Mom and Dad where we're going." They split up, running down two different paths. The rain had stopped, but the clouds hung low, curling their misty fingers around the treetops. Elizabeth smiled. Now it was Peter's turn to prove himself.

A few minutes later, she caught up with the boys at the front gate. The three walked out into the neighborhood, passing a line of neat red brick houses. They stopped at a tall, unclipped hedge.

"This is it," said Peter. He smoothed down his hair with his cupped

---

[3]witch's house

hands, then swung open a high gate. Elizabeth and Jonathan stayed on the sidewalk and peeked through the hedge. The garden was a snarl of vines and plants. In the middle sat a lonely garden bench, with long fingers of grass pressing through the slats.

Elizabeth squinted through the leaves as Peter walked up the brick path. She thought she saw a curtain move, but she couldn't be sure. The front of the house was half hidden by a row of lanky rosebushes. They exploded like fireworks, shooting pink-flowered canes in every direction.

Peter strode up to the front door and knocked firmly. He waited, then knocked again. Finally, he turned to leave, coming down the steps with a shrug and a smile. Just then a scruffy little … something … came yipping around the corner of the house. Elizabeth stood on tiptoe and moved a pair of leaves aside. The *something* was a wire-haired dachshund—with the personality of a great white shark. The dog charged, rocking on its stubby legs. Peter reached the garden bench in one leap. He stood, trapped like a treed squirrel, with the dog snarling and nipping at his ankles.

Suddenly the front door yawned open. A pale round face hovered in the doorway. Even from her place on the sidewalk, Elizabeth could see the slash of dark eyebrows.

Peter raised his hand, as if he were answering a teacher's question. "My good lady," he shouted. "My name is Peter Hoffmann and I would …"

"Maxi!" A deep voice hissed out a command in German. The dog backed into the house, still barking. The door banged shut. Peter stood for a moment, his hand still up in the air. He hopped down and started walking toward the gate. Then he stopped. He turned around, strode to the door, and gave two sharp raps.

"Oh, boy," whispered Jonathan. "I would *never* do that." He ended the sentence with a hiccup as the door creaked open once more.

CHAPTER 11

THE PENDULUM SWINGS

Elizabeth couldn't hear what Peter was saying, but she could see the old woman standing in the doorway. The dog was out of sight, but it was still hammering out angry little yaps. Soon the woman disappeared. She returned wearing a long, dark raincoat. A brown beret, slanted across her forehead, covered one of her eyebrows. With a smile she took Peter's arm and walked down the steps.

Elizabeth shook her head. Her grandmother used to say some people could talk the peel off an orange. The gift of gab, she called it. And Peter had plenty.

"Ah, the Americans. I remember you." As she stepped through the gate, the woman let go of Peter's arm and hooked onto Elizabeth. "I am Frau Kaiser. I will speak to you my English."

Peter and Jonathan followed behind. Elizabeth walked carefully, keeping in step with Frau Kaiser's slow shuffle. "We wanted to ask you something," said Elizabeth. She tried to ignore the reek of mothballs coming from Frau Kaiser's coat. "It's about Professor Vollrath's missing notes. You said your father talked about the notes. Do you think he knew where they were hidden?"

"My father. Yes, he knew many things. Many people. The old ones were telling their stories to him. He would be writing them down." Frau Kaiser gargled her *r*'s with a heavy German accent.

"They say a little creature comes from the river, you know. He finds an open window, then poof ..." She squeezed Elizabeth's arm. "He is jumping into the house. And what mischief he does."

Elizabeth could feel Jonathan's hand poking her in the back. "But the notes," said Elizabeth slowly. "Did your father know anything about Professor Vollrath's notes?"

"The notes? Of course. Oh yes, and he knew where they were. You see, Professor Vollrath was his friend." She began to laugh. "But my father never told *them*." She waved a plump hand in the direction of the observatories. "Oh, no. Never would he tell them."

"But ... did he tell *you*?" Elizabeth stopped walking. The street was silent. No cars. No children's voices. Not even the rustle of a leaf. The whole world seemed to be waiting for the answer.

Frau Kaiser shook her head. "This knowledge he ... how do you say it? He has taken to the grave. He told no one. Not even me."

"But he must have said something. Given some hint."

Frau Kaiser began moving forward again. "He said they are ordinary men with ordinary minds and they look in all the wrong places. And he told me ..." she leaned in close, "on the night with no moon, the wind begins to moan. The ghost of the castle returns."

Elizabeth stiffened. Not another ghost story. She was glad it was daytime. Frau Kaiser had the kind of deep, slow voice she wouldn't want to hear in the dark.

The words droned on. Elizabeth thought about Frau Kaiser's father. He was the one person who knew where Professor Vollrath's notes were hidden. But why didn't he share the secret?

"And when I six years old, my father took me on a ride in an air balloon. I had my birthday, and I wore ..."

Elizabeth gently turned Frau Kaiser around and began walking her back to the house. She shook her head at Jonathan and Peter. They had learned nothing today. Now they were back where they started, with their first and only clue—three dots in the shape of a triangle.

After dinner, the sun broke through the clouds like a fist, bringing a stripe of fresh blue sky. Elizabeth sat in the small kitchen with the rest of the family. She was about to shuffle a deck of cards when she heard Peter's whistle, then footsteps pounding up the stairs. Peter fell into the apartment as she and Jonathan opened the door.

"Ran all the way here," he gasped. "We went for a walk. My parents and I. I went to the maze. Checked the castle door." Peter took a gulp of air. "The hair is broken!" He ran down the stairs. "Come to my house as soon as you can. I have to call Inspector Fischer."

"But, there hasn't been a break-in. Why ..." The door to the guesthouse banged shut. Elizabeth stood at the top of the empty stairway. The pendulum had swung back to the villa burglaries. Things were starting to happen—fast.

Jonathan raced back into the kitchen. "We have to go to Peter's house. All of us. Right away."

Elizabeth spoke just as her father's mouth was forming a question. "We'll explain everything," she said. "Peter needs to call the police."

"Call the police?" asked Mr. Pollack. "Now wait a minute. What's going on?"

"We're gonna catch the villa gang!" shouted Jonathan. "With gobs-of-gum-and-hair. Gobs-of-gum-and-hair." He pranced around the kitchen table, marking each *and hair* by flinging up his arms.

"Jonathan, stop that," said Mrs. Pollack. "I can't even think."

Elizabeth and Jonathan hustled their parents over to Peter's house. The two families took their places in the living room. Jonathan held out a gob of chewing gum and tried to pluck another hair from Elizabeth's ponytail. Peter whirled around the room like a tornado, opening drawers, groping around on shelves. "The card! Where did I put Inspector Fischer's business card?" He ran to his room and came back waving the card in one hand and a cordless phone in the other.

Peter's mother put her hands on his shoulders and gently set him down in an armchair. Peter had some explaining to do. Elizabeth watched the grown-ups as he went over the story again. Mr. Pollack, as usual, was the last to be convinced. He sat with his lips pulled straight, but finally his frown softened.

"I guess it wouldn't hurt to give the information to the police."

Peter shot out of the chair and punched in the phone number as he paced in a circle. "This is Peter Hoffmann," he began, "of the Three Star Detective ... Agency. I'd like to speak to Inspector Fischer. It's about the villa gang and it's urgent."

Elizabeth didn't know what was being said on the other end of the line, but she could see Peter's face getting pink. "This isn't just some tip!" he insisted. "It's the solution to the whole case. I will reveal it to no one but Inspector Fischer himself."

Elizabeth sat stiffly, with an iron grip on the arms of the chair. She wasn't nearly so confident as Peter. And if they were wrong ... But they couldn't be. The police were suspicious of the castle. Why else would they have a look-out at the old observatory? Then someone had mysteriously planted new flowers by the door to the dungeon. And now someone had opened the door, even though it wasn't used any more.

"Yes, I'll be here." Peter hung up the phone. "They're going to try to reach Inspector Fischer and he's going to call us."

Peter tried three different chairs, but he couldn't stay seated. "Oh, man," he muttered. "This is big. Really big." He stood over the phone, like a tiger eyeing its prey.

"I don't know," said Mrs. Pollack. "I'm afraid you kids are in over your heads. This isn't just a mystery. It's a crime. And these people are dangerous."

"I know, Mom, but we didn't ..."

Peter pounced on the telephone at the first jangle. "Hello? Yes, this is Peter Hoffmann." He gave a thumbs-up sign to the others.

Elizabeth wasn't sure how Peter could talk so fast and breathe at the same time. He talked to Inspector Fischer for a long time. She didn't understand everything he said, but she heard him say, "Yes, we're sure" three times, then end with, "No, we'd never make up anything like this."

Peter smiled as he hung up the phone. "He said he's going to try to reach the museum director. He wants to check out what we told him about the door not being used. He said not to go anywhere near the castle tonight. And he might call back."

"Well, no use staring at the phone," said Peter's father. He cleared off a table and brought out a board game. By nine o'clock, there had been no phone call. By ten o'clock, Jonathan was asleep on the table and had to be carried back to the guesthouse.

Elizabeth didn't even try to go to sleep. She picked out her thickest book and read until almost midnight. Finally, her eyes were so heavy, she had to raise her eyebrows to keep them open. She fell into a sleep busy with dreams—blaring sirens, mazes with all dead ends, robbers fleeing through the night. Then, slowly, a deep throbbing sound pushed its way into her dream. Elizabeth woke up in a tremble. Had she heard a helicopter? She lifted her head, listening, frozen. Nothing. She relaxed and drifted back into her dream.

"Look out the window!" Jonathan's shriek tore Elizabeth out of her sleep. She cracked open one eye. At least it was morning. With Jonathan tugging at her arm, she rolled out of bed and stumbled to the window. Without glasses, she could only get a vague hint of the world. The day was sunny. The trees were a green fuzz with no leaves. In the distance was a group of people with no faces.

"Jonathan, I wish I could just wake up in the morning. I mean, without you doing something weird." She leaned out the window and squinted. "And this better be good."

"It *is* good." Jonathan ran into the hallway to alert their parents. "Reporters!" he yelled. "And they're coming this way!"

CHAPTER 12

THE PIRATES' DEN

Reporters? Elizabeth grabbed her glasses. The world came sharply into focus. She could see Peter in full gear. Detective case. White lab coat. He strutted down the path like a peacock with its tail fanned out. Several people were gathered around him, taking notes as he spoke. One of them shouldered a large video camera.

Peter gestured grandly in the direction of the guesthouse. "This is where the American detectives are staying. They've worked on a few important cases in the United States. This is their first case in Germany. I'm sure you'll want to talk to them."

Elizabeth ducked down, crouching under the window sill. Peter was talking about them! A few seconds later she heard footsteps on the stairs to the guesthouse.

Elizabeth sidled over to the bedroom door, then peeked out. If anyone saw her bunny pajamas with the little cotton tail in back, she would have to move to Australia. She grabbed a pair of shorts and a T-shirt and fled into the bathroom.

By the time Elizabeth was dressed, she could hear her parents talking to the reporters. She put her hand on the door handle and took a deep breath. She hoped no one was going to take her picture walking out of the bathroom.

"You're going to be on the news," announced Peter, as she stepped into the hallway. "The whole villa gang is in jail. Four people were arrested last night and another two this morning. We're all supposed to meet Inspector Fischer at the castle. By the old wooden door."

Elizabeth leaned against the wall. She wasn't sure if she was excited or nervous or happy. She only knew it felt like the Fourth of July were being celebrated in her stomach. Jonathan raised his arms and did a few turns around the kitchen table. Mr. and Mrs. Pollack said they had to sit down for a minute.

By the time they all trooped out of the guesthouse, several astronomers were gathered on the steps of the Big Refractor, staring at the strange parade. Peter led his group out the front gate and down the path that ran along outside the observatory park. He kept up a brisk pace, talking as fast as he walked. He made the Three Star Detectives sound like Europe's most important crime fighters.

Soon they neared the castle. The place was brimming with police. After talking to an officer standing in the garden, Peter ducked under a length of yellow police tape. The others followed him through the maze.

Inspector Fischer waited in a patch of sunlight by the door to the dungeon. He waved and motioned the Three Star Detectives to come over. "We've had a full statement from one of the suspects," he whispered. He kept the three next to him as he explained to the reporters what had happened.

Just as they suspected, the burglars had been using the dungeon to store their stolen goods. After each burglary, they would park their car by the old railroad tracks at the bottom of the hill. A narrow footpath led up to the castle. Hidden behind the maze, the old door was the perfect place to enter.

One reporter stepped forward. "How did they get the key to the door? Was one of the museum workers involved?"

"No, nothing like that. One of the gang members posed as a worker and simply walked into the castle. He was able to steal the key, make a copy, then return it the next day. With so many different workers around, no one noticed a thing."

"And the children. What was their role?"

"Their role was vital to solving this case. Of course, we don't recommend that the general public get involved in police investigations. However, these children have exhibited some of the best and ..." he slipped his purple hand into his pocket, "most creative detective work I've ever seen." The minicam swung toward the Three Star Detective Club. Elizabeth looked into the camera and managed a stiff smile, even though her legs trembled so hard she thought her kneecaps would fly off. She was relieved when Inspector Fischer opened the wooden door.

"And now, I will allow you a brief look at what we found inside. Follow me." He carefully felt his way down five stone steps. At the bottom, he turned to Elizabeth. "I want all three of you to wait for me after you come out. I must talk to you about something rather ... surprising." He stared hard in Peter's direction.

Inspector Fischer turned away before Elizabeth could ask any questions. She found herself near the front of the line, with Peter ahead of her and Jonathan behind. She could already hear her brother cooing with delight. As they shuffled down into the cold and damp, the bright summer day went out like a candle. The procession shuffled single file through a dark tunnel-like passageway.

"Be careful, please," called Inspector Fischer. "The floor is uneven, and I'm afraid there may be a few rats in here."

Another gurgle of glee from Jonathan. Elizabeth took small steps, keeping her arms clasped to her sides. She glanced back at her brother. He had better not be getting any stupid ideas. She would have given him a big-sister lip curl, but it was too dark. "Jon, you better not do anything to ..."

"Rat claws," he whispered. Elizabeth felt something stirring in her ponytail. She shook her head wildly, then saw the glow-in-the-dark skeleton hand glimmering on the floor. She stuffed the thing into her pocket and shoved Jonathan in front of her.

Elizabeth wasn't sure who was behind her now or where her parents were. She could hear no voices, only the scraping of feet as the group trudged deeper into the dungeon. Blinking into the gloom, she could see three empty doorways on the left. Each opened into a dim cell that sent an icy breath of air into the passageway. Elizabeth rubbed her arms, but it didn't do any good. Her whole body bristled with goose bumps.

"Step aside, please. Video camera coming through." A shock of light cut into the darkness, as if the noonday sun had suddenly come out at midnight. In the glare, the ancient walls glistened with trickling water. Straight ahead Elizabeth could see a stone wall with a thick iron ring. "I bet that's where they chained the prisoners," said Jonathan. His voice didn't sound gleeful anymore.

The light from the camera swung to the right as the passageway turned sharply. Inspector Fischer stopped in front of an open door and the others crowded in behind him. Yellow police tape stretched across the opening. As the light from the camera flooded the tiny room, Elizabeth heard a whistle, which must have been Peter, and a hiccup, which must have been Jonathan. The tiny cell was a pirates' den of treasure. Along the wall crates spilled over with loot—jewelry with sparkling stones of every color, gold statues, silver plates, silver candlesticks, coin collections, even some swords and old-fashioned pistols.

"Please take a look and then move along," said Inspector Fischer. "So everyone gets a chance to see." With no room for the Outer Mongolian Warrior Dance, Jonathan hopped up and down in place. "Gobs-of-gum-and-hair," he chanted. "Gobs-of-gum-and-hair." Elizabeth finally pulled him away and guided him back down the passageway with Peter behind them. On the way out, the three squeezed past their parents, who were at the end of the line. "Wait 'til you see what's in there," said Peter. "This is big. Really big."

Elizabeth hurried down the passageway, heading for the open door. She bounded out into the sunlight, stretching out her arms to gather up the warmth. She thought about her friends in Indiana. And about their grandfather, Pop. Right this very minute, they were all the way on the other side of the earth, probably still sleeping. What would they think if they knew Elizabeth and Jonathan Pollack, ace detectives, had just helped the police catch a gang of jewel thieves?

Elizabeth stepped to the side when she saw the cameraman come out of the dungeon. Jonathan danced around, still babbling about chewing gum and hair. The cameraman bent down and took a close-up of the gum on the door.

Finally, one by one, the reporters left. Inspector Fischer came out of the dungeon and left two policemen guarding the door. He walked through the maze with the three detectives and their parents. When they reached the fountain in the middle, he motioned to Elizabeth, Jonathan, and Peter. "We need to talk," he said. "Sit down for a minute." He nodded to their parents. "I'll bring them right back. You can wait for us in the garden."

Elizabeth squeezed onto the end of the bench, letting Peter sit next to Jonathan. Inspector Fischer sat on the edge of the fountain, facing them. His mouth looked small and tight. Elizabeth knew enough about grown-ups to realize this wasn't a good sign. "You've done excellent detective work," he said. "Noticing the new flowers was the key to everything. I can't think of any detective who would have been so clever. And the idea of the hair was, uh, not exactly what the police would have done, but it worked." He hesitated. Here it comes, thought Elizabeth. What had they done wrong now?

"There's something I didn't tell the press. Did you notice a man in the park, always drinking out of a bottle?"

"Of course," said Peter. "I knew right away he was an undercover agent. He should get a better disguise. It didn't fool me for a minute."

"You're a clever boy, Peter. And you're right, the man was in disguise. But there's only one problem. He wasn't a policeman. He was a member of the villa gang."

"He was what?" Elizabeth felt like someone had dropped a bowling ball into her stomach.

"He was a member of the gang. He came to the garden as a look-out. They were afraid the police were getting suspicious. He was sent to keep an eye out and see if the police were snooping around. He posed as a drinker who came to the park every day. He told us the whole story last night."

A tidal wave of red swept over Peter's face. Even his freckles disappeared. "And I even talked to him once. I told him we were there for the same reason."

"Exactly," said Inspector Fischer. "He told me he didn't think much about it, but then he heard two old women talking about you. He realized that you children were snooping around the castle door and he got worried. Yesterday the gang decided they had to find a new hiding place. That's why they were in the castle last night. They were going to start moving things out. If they had succeeded, that could have ruined our investigation." He looked at them sternly. "You made one big mistake. And that was not telling us as soon as you suspected something."

"I just wanted to be sure," said Elizabeth in a small voice, "before we bothered you again."

Inspector Fischer stood up and shook hands with each of them. "All's well that ends well, my friends. But next time, don't try to do everything by yourselves."

By the time the morning was over, Elizabeth had lost count of how many times they told their story. Every astronomer suddenly wanted to know all about the Three Star Detective Club. Even the director of Observatory Hill called them into her office.

Just before noon, the Pollack family said good-bye to Peter and his parents. Elizabeth trudged toward the guesthouse. Her voice was hoarse. Her stomach roared like a lion, reminding her she hadn't eaten any breakfast.

"I see something!" Jonathan tore away from the others and scooped up a brightly wrapped package sitting on the steps of the guesthouse. He gave the box an expert sniff, then clutched it to his chest as he scampered up the stairs. Elizabeth opened a card that had fallen off the gift.

> Please excuse us for not trusting you. We did not realize you were detectives working on a case.
>
> The Rose Garden Ladies

Elizabeth raced up after Jonathan and followed him into their bedroom. "It's from the two ladies who were spying on us at the castle. And whatever it is, we're supposed to share." She pried a box of chocolate-covered cherries out of his hands. Jonathan managed to grab two.

"My breakfast." Jonathan popped one candy into each cheek, then squeezed his face with his hands. He gave his sister a chocolate-covered grin.

"Jonathan, can't you do *anything* without being weird?" Elizabeth flopped into a chair. She could hear noises of lunch being prepared in the kitchen. She was too tired to get up and help.

"Pishers," said Jonathan. He had taken two more cherries. He swallowed. "Pictures. They're done already." He wiped his hands on his pants and picked up the photos. "Here's the one by the castle door. We were standing right there. And we didn't even know the robbers were using it." Jonathan picked up a magnifying glass.

"If you're looking for bacteria, I don't want to know about it." Elizabeth leaned back and closed her eyes.

"Hey, you gotta see this," said Jonathan.

Elizabeth kept her eyes squeezed shut. Maybe if she just ignored him ...

"You *gotta* see this." He pumped her arm up and down. "The castle door has three bolts."

"So?"

"Like the clue. Three dots. Three bolts. In a triangle."

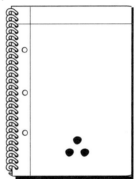

"Yeah, except the hidden notes don't have anything to do with the castle. And anyway, I can't think about another mystery right now. We already ..."

Elizabeth sat up slowly and stared at a blank spot on the wall. "The other picture," she muttered. "I've got to see the other picture."

She leaped off the bed, grabbed the photo and the magnifying glass, and raced toward the door.

"You're a fantastic detective, Jonathan," she yelled. She disappeared down the stairs. "And the best brother in the world!"

Jonathan ran to the door and peered down the empty stairway. "I am?"

CHAPTER 13

A GHOSTLY TALE

Jonathan caught up with Elizabeth just as she slipped through the heavy doors of the Administration Building. He trotted after her down the dim corridor. "I don't get it. How come I'm so great?"

"I'll tell you in a minute. First we have to go in the library."

They pushed open the doors and tiptoed into the room. Elizabeth didn't have to tell Jonathan to be quiet. The stern leather books, lining the walls from floor to ceiling, commanded silence. Elizabeth felt like she should be walking around on cotton balls.

A few scientists looked up from their books and computer screens and spoke to each other behind their hands. Elizabeth hoped to find Peter's mother, but the desk by the door was empty. She gave a weak smile to the upturned heads, then remembered the Top Ten Tips for Detectives. Number 6. *Never look uncertain. Always act as if you know what you're doing.*

"Follow me, Jon," she whispered. "And don't touch anything." Elizabeth strode across the room with a slight swing of her arms. If Peter could walk like a peacock, she could too. As she tapped up the spiral staircase to the upper level, she could practically feel the curious stares burning a hole in her back.

She led Jonathan along the metal walkway that circled the room high above the main floor. "This is it. The display about Professor

Vollrath. And here's the picture we need to look at." Elizabeth carefully opened the glass case. She held the magnifying glass up to the picture of Professor Vollrath standing by a brick wall. "Perfect."

Jonathan stretched up and stared at the picture. "But it's just Professor Vollrath standing in front of his house."

"False assumption. That's what I thought too. But it couldn't be." She handed Jonathan the magnifying glass. "Look at the wall where he's standing. The pattern of the brick. And then look at the picture of us at the castle."

"It's the same. That—what do you call it—flaming bond or something."

"Flemish bond, I think. The bricks were laid long side, short side, long side, short side. Peter said the castle is the only building around with that pattern."

"I get it! Professor Vollrath was standing by the castle wall. And that dark part at the edge of the picture is the door to the dungeon."

"Right. And look at that big key in his hand. I bet it's the key to the old door. It all makes sense. Professor Vollrath helped start the castle museum. That's probably why he had the key."

"You mean I was right about the three bolts on the door? That's the clue of the three dots?"

"I think it is."

Jonathan suddenly forgot about being quiet. He began to blare out his words like a trumpet. "So Professor Vollrath hid his notes in the dungeon!" Elizabeth cupped her hand over Jonathan's mouth, muffling the words into *Professor Vollrath hid his nose in the dustbin.*

"Don't start yelling about it," she hissed. "We're not even sure yet. We need to talk to Professor Bergstrom—both of them. And Peter too." She closed the glass case and tried to creep out of the library unnoticed, but it didn't work. She walked down the winding stairs and waded into a sea of curious eyes. "Just another case," said Elizabeth with a wave of her hand.

She strode out of the library with Jonathan behind her. As soon as the door clicked shut, her stomach gave a growl the size of New York City. She and Jonathan looked at each other. Lunch!

Jonathan bounded up the stairs of the guesthouse ahead of Elizabeth. "Don't say anything about the missing notes," she called. "We'll surprise them later."

After a quick meal, Jonathan and Elizabeth raced around the corner to the white stucco house. "Peter first," said Elizabeth. She rang the bell to the second floor apartment but found out that Peter was busy. He was showing his "detective lab" to a reporter from the local newspaper. Elizabeth stepped over to the Bergstrom's door and rang the first floor bell. Jonathan did a dance on the doormat. "Three dots on the dungeon door," he chanted.

Just as Elizabeth was about to ring the doorbell again, she heard the shuffle of footsteps. Mrs. Bergstrom opened the door.

"The two famous detectives! What a nice surprise." She motioned them to come in. "*Everyone* is talking about you. This is the most exciting thing that's happened since ... since the comet struck Jupiter." Leaning on her cane, she led them into a sitting room sprinkled with books and piles of knitting. The room reminded Elizabeth of her grandfather's house. Quiet and cozy. The way a place gets when it's been exactly the same for a very long time. She and Jonathan each sank into a soft armchair.

"I had no idea you were working with the police on those burglaries," said Mrs. Bergstrom. "You must tell me all about it." She lowered herself onto a small sofa and leaned her cane on the wall.

"Well, actually," said Elizabeth, "we're here to talk about something else. We had a new idea about finding the missing notes. It's ... well, this sounds weird, but has anyone ever looked at the castle?"

"The castle? No, I'm sure no one has looked there. We had no reason. And also, the castle is so big. Where would one look?"

Jonathan piped up. "Three dots on the dungeon door!"

"The dungeon door?" repeated Mrs. Bergstrom.

Elizabeth explained how the clues seemed to point to the castle dungeon. The three bolts on the castle door in the form of a triangle, the picture of Professor Vollrath standing by that same door, and the large key in his hand.

As she was talking, Mr. Bergstrom slipped into the room. Without saying a word, he nodded hello and sat next to wife. As he listened to Elizabeth, he cradled a pipe in his hands but didn't smoke it.

"Is it crazy to think the notes might be hidden in the dungeon?" asked Elizabeth.

"I don't think it's at all crazy. What do you think, Olaf?"

"I think," he said, "that I owe this young man a ghost story." He pointed his pipe at Jonathan. "I promised to tell you one last week and I never did."

"Oh. Uh, sure."

"You know, I quite like riding the bus," he began. "I get some exercise walking to the bus stop, I'm not polluting the air with a car, and I meet some interesting people."

"Right." Elizabeth tried to sound interested, but she wanted to talk about the missing notes, not ghosts or riding the bus.

Mr. Bergstrom continued. "I sometimes meet a woman on the bus. A woman who knows many stories about this place."

Jonathan sneaked a look at Elizabeth then turned to Mr. Bergstrom. "Does the lady on the bus have kind of ... dark eyebrows?"

"Yes, her eyebrows are different, you might say. Actually, I think they are painted on." Mr. Bergstrom sat back, putting his hands on his knees. "The old woman told me a story once. A ghostly tale. On the nights with no moon, she said, a ghost comes to haunt the castle. A wind begins to blow, softly at first, then stronger and stronger. It carries the sound of screams and cries. The sound of a struggle. And that's when one hears the footsteps scraping along the dungeon floor. Back and forth. Back and forth."

"Olaf, I really don't think ..." began Mrs. Bergstrom.

Her husband held up his hand. "Please let me finish. I think you will find it very interesting. The woman told me this is the ghost of a man who was once a prisoner in the dungeon. He was the only prisoner ever to escape. Unfortunately, he had only one week of freedom. He was caught and dragged back to the dungeon, screaming and crying out for help."

Elizabeth's hands gripped the arms of the chair. Why in the world was he telling them this?

"Now, comes the important part. You see, his escape had been cleverly planned. His family had smuggled a knife and a length of rope to him in a most unexpected way—baked into two loaves of bread. With these tools he was able to overpower and tie up the guard, then escape through the door in the castle wall."

Mr. Bergstrom paused, looking at each of them in turn. "According to the story, the prisoner had removed a loose stone in the wall of his cell and carved out a hiding place behind it, a hiding place big enough to keep his weapon and his rope."

And big enough, thought Elizabeth, to hide Professor Vollrath's notebooks. She began to get the Fourth of July feeling in her stomach again.

"But is the story true?" asked Mrs. Bergstrom. "Was there really such a prisoner?"

"That I do not know," said her husband. "But legends are often partly based on fact."

"I get it," said Jonathan. "The hiding place is real. And Professor Vollrath knew about it." Jonathan popped out of his chair. "So he hid his notes in there and we can go find them."

"Maybe," said Mr. Bergstrom. "It is possible that Professor Vollrath knew about the story and found the hiding place. Yes, this is an interesting idea. It explains the clue of the three dots. It explains why the notes were never found."

"Excuse me. I must do something." Mrs. Bergstrom picked up her cane and walked out of the living room, closing the door behind her.

Elizabeth sat on the edge of her chair. How could the Bergstroms be calm, just when they were so close to solving the mystery? Mr. Bergstrom stretched out his legs and lit his pipe. He took a few quiet puffs. "Anna told me of your grandfather's idea about a false assumption. Now I think perhaps he is right. You see, everyone assumed the notes were hidden on Observatory Hill. The idea seemed logical. This is where Professor Vollrath lived and worked. But the assumption has kept us from looking in other places. All these years." He shook his head. "A scientist must learn to question all assumptions. We did not follow our own rules. But it is never too late."

"Two cases in one day!" Jonathan flopped back onto the chair and thrust his arms up into a V. Elizabeth smiled, then suddenly felt her forehead tighten, the same way her father's did when something bothered him.

"Wait. There's one thing I don't get. Why would Professor Vollrath hide his notes so far away? Walk all the way to the castle. Go in the dungeon."

"Excellent," said Mr. Bergstrom. "Good questions, Elizabeth, are the mark of a good scientist. We must try to understand Professor Vollrath. He hid the notes only when he went away, which was not often. But still, why would he go to so much trouble?" Mr. Bergstrom paused and studied his pipe. "I did not know Professor Vollrath, but many years ago, I spoke to an astronomer who did. Professor Vollrath was ... well, he was a good scientist but he became strange. He spoke of spies who would try to steal his work. Eventually he trusted no one, not even his friends. So yes, I can imagine how he could have ..."

The buzz of the doorbell broke into his sentence. Once. Twice. Three times. Mr. Bergstrom rose from the couch. "Our friend Peter is here."

Peter burst into the room like a strong gust of wind. "There's going to be a big story about us in the newspaper tomorrow. They even took pictures of my detective lab. Three junior detectives solve the villa burglaries." Peter gave a proud smile, but all eyes turned to Mrs. Bergstrom as she walked in.

"You'll need to wear your warmest clothes," she said. "And bring flashlights. I just spoke to the director of the museum. There is only one way to test our theory. Tomorrow morning we go to the castle." She raised her eyebrows. "A special tour of the dungeon."

CHAPTER 14

DOWN IN THE DUNGEON

"I am *not* going until you empty your pockets." Elizabeth crossed her arms and stood over her brother. If Sherlock Holmes had worked with an assistant like Jonathan, he would have run away and joined the circus. "I'm not kidding, Jon."

Jonathan stuck out his tongue as he snapped open two pockets at the side of his pants. He pulled out a fake spider, his rubber vomit, and a giant rubber cockroach.

"And if you bring that stupid skeleton hand into the dungeon again, I'll … I'll …" Elizabeth was running out of threats. That's what came of having a brother like Jonathan. "I'll throw it in the river."

A few minutes later Elizabeth and Jonathan walked into the kitchen bundled up in sweatshirts and jackets. Their parents were still eating breakfast.

"I don't understand why you're taking a tour of the dungeon," said Mr. Pollack. "We just saw the dungeon yesterday. There's not much down there, now that all the loot is gone."

"Well, we have a reason," said Elizabeth, "but we can't tell you until later. It's a surprise." She glanced out the window and saw Peter coming up the steps. He didn't whistle. He didn't take two steps at a time. And he rang the doorbell once, not three times. Elizabeth wasn't surprised. The evening news on television didn't exactly make Peter into a star. The video showed the treasure stashed in the dungeon and not much else. Peter had to be content with a two-second shot of the back of his head.

"The newspaper story was good," said Elizabeth as she and Jonathan headed down the stairs to meet him.

"I guess, but it was on page three. I thought we would make the headlines." Peter shrugged. "My mom says I expect too much."

Just as they walked out the door, the Bergstrom's tiny white car pulled up in front of the guesthouse. The three detectives squeezed into the back seat.

"We have special permission to drive into the courtyard," said Mr. Bergstrom. "Because of Anna's knees." He waved to the guard as they drove out the gate of Observatory Hill. They bumped down a narrow street and soon arrived at the castle. When Elizabeth saw the lonely courtyard she realized it was Saturday. The castle stood waiting for them. Completely empty.

The dim haze of mystery brings old and new together. Elizabeth thought about the strange message in the fortune cookie. The new mystery of the villa burglaries. The old mystery of the missing notes. And the castle. The castle was where they came together.

"I'm afraid the dungeon is no place for an old lady with bad knees," said Mrs. Bergstrom. "Peter will walk me through the maze, and I'll wait for you outside. When you get down to the dungeon, open the old wooden door to the outside. We'll be right there."

As Peter and Mrs. Bergstrom set off across the bridge, the others walked up to the huge double doors of the castle. A brass lion's head with a thick ring in its mouth glared down at them. Jonathan stood on tiptoe and gave two mighty raps. Slowly the door swung open.

"Welcome." A bearded man in a suit and tie waved them in. "Helmut Brandt. Museum Director." He shook hands with each of them. "Mrs. Bergstrom tells me you think some scientific papers may be hidden in the dungeon."

"We're sure they are," said Elizabeth. "All the clues fit."

"Yes. Well, I must say I know nothing of a hiding place in the dungeon, but you're welcome to search. Especially two such well-known detectives."

Herr Brandt[4] led them into a cavernous hall littered with crates and boxes and tools. Jonathan wandered over to a fireplace so big he could walk into it without bending. Herr Brandt led them across the stone floor to a small arched door.

"These will be our new exhibit rooms." He opened the door to a long room with a high ceiling. Sunlight spilled onto the shiny wood floor through a row of tall windows. "This used to be the ballroom," he said. "And some people say, if you stare into the mirrors on the wall you can still see the dancers." Elizabeth looked up at the huge mirrors in their fancy gold frames. She had no trouble imagining couples sweeping by in puffy silks and satins.

They walked through a doorway into another long empty room. Then another. And another. No one spoke. All Elizabeth could hear were their footsteps tapping like hammers as they walked through the empty rooms. They were walking the entire length of the castle. Finally, they reached the last room, with a low ceiling and dark paneling on the walls.

Herr Brandt stopped in front of the far wall. "This is not on our regular tours," he laughed. "But it is here the treasure hunt begins." He took out a small key and suddenly a wooden panel on the wall sprang open. A secret door! Elizabeth peeked over his shoulder to see a set of stone steps twisting down into the darkness. Herr Brandt clicked a light mounted on the wall.

"I must ask you to hold onto the railing," he said. "The steps are very narrow." Elizabeth walked in front of Jonathan and held on with both hands, carefully feeling her way down each tiny step.

The stairs spiraled down, farther and farther, until Elizabeth felt

---

[4]Herr is the word for Mister in German.

they must have reached the center of the earth. Then, at the bottom, a rough wooden door announced the entrance to the dungeon.

"This is the end of the electric light," said Herr Brandt. He clicked on a large flashlight and gave the door a push. As the dungeon door opened, the damp air reached out like a cold hand. Elizabeth stepped into the darkness. The place seemed different today. No policemen. No reporters. And no bright light from the camera. Elizabeth thought about the rose garden, bright and fragrant with flowers. Here in the dungeon it was never warm. Never summer.

At first Elizabeth wasn't sure where she was, then she realized they had walked in at the end of the passage. They stood right next to the room where the loot was found. She could still see a scrap of yellow police tape hanging from the doorway.

They made their way to the other end of the passage and opened the door for Peter. Mrs. Bergstrom waved at them and stayed outside.

"Oh, man. I love this place." Peter stepped down into the passageway and peered into the first cell.

"There are five rooms," said Herr Brandt. "Let's search them one by one and stay together. I had a small ladder brought down for us."

They started in the cell nearest to the outside door. The uneven stones in the passageway gave way to a hard-packed dirt floor. A tiny slit of a window gave a glimpse of blue sky. They stood in a line and felt along the rough stone walls. Nothing budged. Peter stepped on the ladder and felt as high as he could reach. "Nothing up here," he reported.

They repeated the search in each of the cells.

"I was afraid this would be the result," said Herr Brandt. "We haven't done much with the dungeon, but surely someone would have noticed a loose stone. And the legend you mentioned. I've never heard anything about that." He shined his light on his watch.

We can't just give up, thought Elizabeth. We need more time.

Maybe that's why grown-ups didn't always find things. They were always in a hurry.

"Is this the only dungeon?" she asked. "The only place they kept prisoners?"

"That's right. There's nothing under the rest of the castle."

"Well … could you wait while I talk to Mrs. Bergstrom?" Elizabeth ran out the door. Mrs. Bergstrom was sitting on a little folding stool.

"You found nothing," she said. "I can tell from your face."

"We looked in all the cells. There are no loose stones. No hiding places." Elizabeth looked again at the heavy wooden door. Three bolts. One on top and two on the bottom, just like in the clue. They had figured everything out, but something was still missing.

"We are not going to give up so easily," said Mrs. Bergstrom. "I have an idea. Call the others out here please."

The searchers sat on the grass in the sunshine.

"Olaf, you must go to Frau Kaiser's house. Ask her to tell you the story again. Maybe there's a detail you have forgotten."

Herr Brandt looked at his watch again. He said he would wait in his office, but he had to leave by noon.

Mr. Bergstrom disappeared into the maze. "I'll be back soon," he called.

"Well, I'm waiting out here." Jonathan laid his head back on the soft grass. "The sky looks pretty when you lay on your back and look up at it."

Pretty? Elizabeth narrowed her eyes. Jonathan rarely did anything that didn't have something to do with his quest for the disgusting.

"I used to love to lie down on the grass and watch the sky," said Mrs. Bergstrom, "and I would join you if I wasn't so old."

Peter stretched out on the grass next to Jonathan. Elizabeth lay down on the other side. Her brother was right. The sky looked as wide and blue as the open sea. A cotton candy cloud wandered by. Elizabeth remembered a game she used to play with her father, trying to imagine what animal the clouds looked like.

"Looks like a giant rat." Jonathan sat up. "I saw a rat in the dungeon, you know. It went into a little hole in the wall. The one with the ring in it."

Elizabeth closed her eyes and lay perfectly still. She didn't want Jonathan to start going on about rats.

By the time Mr. Bergstrom returned, she was almost asleep. "What a treasure I've found!"

She shot up. "Treasure?"

"Frau Kaiser. Did you know that her father collected stories from all the old people in the area? Fairy tales. Legends. He wrote down some of them, and the others she knows by heart. She does get a little confused and repeats herself, but the stories—she remembers all of them. Word for word."

"My mom calls people like that memory keepers," said Elizabeth. "People that save pieces of the past. And she says you can never solve an old mystery unless you get their help."

"Exactly," said Mr. Bergstrom. "So I asked her about the prisoner story. It *was* a story Professor Vollrath knew. He was the one she heard it from. She told me the story again, and I wrote everything down. But I don't think it's much different." He pulled a sheet of paper from his pocket. "She said the man was a prisoner in a dark dungeon room and he was the only person ever to escape. His family gave him two loaves of bread, one with a knife baked inside and one with a piece of rope. He was able to loosen a stone in the wall and carve out a hiding place."

"I guess that's what you said before," said Elizabeth. "Except the part about the dungeon room being *dark*. I don't think you said that before. But it seems like they're all pretty dark."

Herr Brandt appeared in the doorway to the dungeon. "I heard your car pull into the courtyard. Any new ideas?"

"I'm not sure," said Mrs. Bergstrom. "But could you just let them take one more look? And then I promise we won't bother you again."

Elizabeth zipped up her jacket and followed the others as they shuffled down the steps into the dungeon. They looked again in each cell, but they discovered nothing new. Jonathan lost interest after the second room. He went into the passageway with Peter. Elizabeth could hear them discussing rats.

"There's something strange here," called Peter.

"Yeah, and his name is Jonathan Pollack," shouted Elizabeth.

"Really," said Jonathan. "You gotta see this." Elizabeth gritted her teeth and marched out of the cell with Mr. Bergstrom and Herr Brandt. The two boys stood at the end of the passageway in front of the wall with the iron ring. "The rat went in right there," said Jonathan, pointing to a spot near his foot.

"But there's something else you need to look at," said Peter. He held his own flashlight in one hand and Jonathan's in the other. "There's a row of stones missing. Up there." He directed the light to the top of the wall. It was short of the ceiling by about a foot.

"Yes, we're not sure about that," said Herr Brandt. "For some reason, the wall was never completed." He looked at Mr. Bergstrom. "Do you think you need much more time? I'm afraid I have appointments this afternoon."

Elizabeth shined her flashlight to the top of the wall. She couldn't see much. But something … something wasn't right.

"Can you wait just a minute, Herr Brandt? I don't know. I need to think." She turned to Jonathan. "Were you telling the truth about seeing that rat?"

"Sure I was. I don't lie. I just find weird stuff all the time. That's my job." He took Elizabeth's flashlight and shined it on a wide crack at the bottom of the wall.

Mr. Bergstrom leaned over and examined the spot. "I think I know what's bothering you, Elizabeth. Why would a rat go through a wall into solid rock? Unless ..."

"Unless there was something behind the wall," said Elizabeth. She could already hear Jonathan dancing up and down.

Herr Brandt gave the ring a hard tug. Nothing happened. Elizabeth took off her jacket and looped it around the ring. As they all pulled, a scraping sound echoed in the darkness.

"A door!" yelled Peter. "There's a door in the wall."

Elizabeth picked up her flashlight. She held on tight with both hands, aiming it at the wall. The quivering light showed a door, half open, cut into the stone. And behind the door—nothing but darkness.

"I had no idea," said the director. "Absolutely no idea." He put his hand on Peter's arm. "Let me go in first. I ... I'm not sure what I'm going to find in there." Herr Brandt turned sideways and slipped through the opening. Elizabeth was glad she had a ponytail. Otherwise her hair would probably be standing on end.

"It's empty," he called. "You can come in."

They stepped into a small room with no windows. The flashlights did little to brighten the gloom. The place was black as midnight, as if the stones themselves were made of darkness.

"The missing stones at the top were meant to let some air in," said Herr Brandt, "but not light."

"It's not fair," said Jonathan. Elizabeth couldn't see his face, but his voice sounded quivery, just like it did when he went down in the last round of the Geography Bee. "It's not fair to keep someone in here. In the dark. I hate it. And I'm going outside."

"Jon, wait." Elizabeth moved toward the door. She wanted to go after Jonathan, but she hated to leave. They had finally reached the very heart of the mystery.

"I'll go with him," said Peter. "It's okay. You figured out most of this case anyway. So you should do the search. I'll tell Mrs. Bergstrom what's going on." He ran after Jonathan. "Wait for me. I'll race you through the maze."

Elizabeth stood in the middle of the room. This was the *dark room* in Frau Kaiser's story. She was sure. Mr. Brandt held the flashlight as she felt along the wall. The stones were the same as in the other cells. Rough. Cold. Then, in the middle of the second wall, Elizabeth pushed on a stone just like the others. But this time the stone answered back with a scraping sound. And slightly, ever so slightly, it moved.

CHAPTER 15

HIDDEN TREASURE

That night, a stream of visitors made their way through the darkness to the Big Refractor Observatory. Elizabeth stood on the steps with Jonathan and her parents. She recognized some of the astronomers in the group. And Peter's parents, of course. Karl walked up with Professor Klein, the woman who was the director of Observatory Hill. Even Inspector Fischer showed up. Each had gotten a mysterious phone call from the Bergstroms.

Peter glowed in his white lab coat. He scurried up and down the steps, greeting newcomers and herding the group together.

Suddenly the giant doors swung open from the inside. Mr. Bergstrom appeared in a stream of light. "Good. I see our group is assembled. Please come in." He led them through a large room, then up a steep spiral stairway.

Elizabeth was at the front of the line. At the top of the stairs, she stepped through a doorway onto a gleaming wood floor. She found herself in a simple round room with the dome cupped high overhead. All around the circle, just above her head, were the small wheels and pulleys that opened the dome.

Elizabeth moved aside to let the others in. All eyes were drawn to the star of the show. In the middle of the room the Big Refractor telescope towered above them, smooth and sleek as an arrow. The dome was open and the tip of the telescope pointed out into the night.

"Clear skies and no moon," said Mr. Bergstrom. "We have

an exceptional view of Jupiter tonight." He pointed to a computer humming softly on a desk next to the telescope. On the screen an image of the planet shimmered in shades of gray. "You see, we no longer look directly through the telescope but instead view the images on the computer screen."

Elizabeth could see Professor Klein exchange puzzled looks with the other astronomers. Why had they been called here?

Mr. Bergstrom turned to the side and held out one arm. His wife shuffled out from behind the telescope, looking small and frail next to the huge instrument.

The director strode up to greet her. "Professor Bergstrom! You haven't been up here in years."

"This is a special day," said Mrs. Bergstrom. "A day when all things are possible." She turned to Inspector Fischer. "I have news that will surprise you, Inspector. When the police removed all the stolen goods from the dungeon, they left the most important treasure behind."

Inspector Fischer stared at Mrs. Bergstrom. An uncertain smile flickered across his face.

Mrs. Bergstrom stood next to Elizabeth, Jonathan, and Peter. She held up a large canvas bag. "Because of the enquiring minds of these three clever young detectives, we were able to find a hidden treasure." As she opened the bag, Elizabeth removed a large bundle. She turned to the director and handed her a tattered wad of newspapers, black with mold and dirt. Professor Klein took the bundle and held it at arm's length, keeping it away from the trim gray suit she wore. "But I don't know why ..."

Mr. Bergstrom brought over a small table. "I think you will be interested to see what's inside, Professor."

As the others crowded around her, Professor Klein put the newspaper on the table and slowly opened the layers of brittle paper. The last page unfolded to reveal two slim volumes of spotted brown leather. The director opened to the first page, stiff and warped with dampness.

"*Professor Heinrich Vollrath,*" she read. "*Hamburg Observatory, 1919.*" She looked up. "But how can this be? These have been missing for over eighty years!"

Peter raised his hand, about to speak, but Mrs. Bergstrom shook her head at him. She gently pushed Elizabeth forward. "This is your story to tell."

Elizabeth looked at the grown-ups. Every eye was focused on her. She wanted to begin, but her mind had gone as blank as a stone. "Well, we just ... we just ..."

"Tell 'em how I figured out the three dots," whispered Jonathan.

Elizabeth nodded. She began the story slowly. The clue of the three dots. Jonathan noticing the bolts on the castle door. The legend of the ghost. The search of the castle. By the time she had reached the part about the hidden dungeon room, she could see everything in her mind as she spoke. She could feel the rough stone moving slightly, then inching out as she pulled, until the heavy stone slid right out into her hands.

"And there really was a space behind the stone," she said, "just like in the story. The notes were there, all wrapped up in newspaper." Elizabeth stopped and caught her breath.

For a moment, the grown-ups were silent. Then, Mr. Pollack raised his hands and began to clap. Soon the whole room filled with applause. Elizabeth and Jonathan stood stiff and smiling. Peter waved and took a bow.

Elizabeth told the story again and again, but after awhile, she found herself standing alone. Her father was having a lively conversation with an astronomer about deep space. Her mother and Mr. Bergstrom discussed how to get someone from the University to meet with Frau Kaiser and write down her stories.

Elizabeth looked for the other two Star Detectives. Jonathan, with his extra large rubber vomit in his hand, had actually managed to find someone interested in looking at it. And Peter, as bold as a bullfrog, was begging Professor Klein to disconnect the computer from the telescope so he could look through the eyepiece.

Mrs. Bergstrom put her hand on Elizabeth's shoulder. "Those two boys are a bit much to handle," she said. "I know. I grew up with four brothers. One thing you can be sure of, my dear. Your life will never be dull."

"But I guess we won't see Peter again after we go back to Indiana."

"I wouldn't be so sure of that," said Mrs. Bergstrom. "I have the feeling the Three Star Detective Club hasn't seen its last mystery."

Elizabeth swallowed hard. Peter the Great. Jonathan the Annoying. It could be a wild ride. She had better learn to hang on tight.

BE A WORLD EXPLORER

Jonathan and Elizabeth find mystery and adventure in Germany, but you don't have to travel to explore the world. There are lots of ways to get to know another country—books, videos, pictures, family stories, recipes.

How can *you* be a world explorer? First of all, choose a country. It could be a country one of your parents or grandparents or great-great-great-grandparents came from. It could be a place someone in your family has visited. Or a place that a friend is from. Or just a place that interests you.

After you've chosen your country—

1. Look at a globe or a world atlas at home or at the library. Find out exactly where your special country is located.

2. Find out more. Where? Look in your library for a children's atlas or an encyclopedia. The library may also have a book or a video about that country. Perhaps one of your parents can help you find information on the Internet.

3. Draw a picture of the flag.

4. Find out about the wildlife in your special country. Do they have animals or plants that are different from ours? Germany, for example, has hedgehogs, which we don't.

5. Find a story or a children's book about that country. Ask a librarian to help you.

6. Find out what special holidays are celebrated in that country. If you want, you could make that day a special day in your family.

7.   Be a cook! Every country has its own special foods. There are cookbooks at the library and recipes on the Internet. You might even have some family recipes. Write down a recipe and give it a try.

8.   Find out if anyone in your family has stories about visiting or living in that country.

9.   Learn some words from that country. How? Look for a dictionary at the library. Or check out the "Say Hello to the World" Internet site, sponsored by the Internet Public Library. Here's how to say "Hello" in four different languages:

German: Guten Tag   GOO-ten tahk (Good day)
Japanese: Konichiwa   Koh-NEE-chee-wah
Swahili: Jambo   JAHM-bo
Spanish: Hola   OH-la

10.   Be a word detective. Find out about English words that came from your country's language. Did you know that the word *rodeo* came from Spanish, *safari* came from Swahili, *karate* is a Japanese word, and *kindergarten* is a German word?

ABOUT THE AUTHOR

Eleanor Rosellini grew up in Park Ridge, Illinois, and attended the University of Illinois and Indiana University. In writing her stories of long-lost treasure, she draws on the people and places of her own family history, as well as her extensive travels in Germany. Interested in both history and ecology, she is active in a variety of environmental initiatives and currently gives walking tours of historic Boston. She lives in Massachusetts with her husband and two children. Visit her at www.hiddentreasuremysteries.com

BOOKS OF INTEREST

Also by Eleanor Rosellini, an excerpt from *The Puzzle in the Portrait* ...

A Puzzling Phone Call

July 12th. Williams Bay, Wisconsin. Just arrived at grandfather's house. Brother is running around birdbath, waving a stick and grunting like a cave man.

Elizabeth Pollack smiled as she closed her journal. Someday she would write a book about her brother. No doubt about it. Jonathan had to be shared with the world.

She slid out of the car and watched. Jonathan was definitely a challenge. He had just turned eight, and was restless and wiry. And nosy as a raccoon. Elizabeth put on her big-sister voice. "Would you quit snorting? You're scaring the chipmunks." Jonathan came to a stop and raised the stick in the air. His sandy brown hair stood on end, whipped up by a stiff summer breeze. "An ancient warrior dance!" he shouted. "From Outer Mongolia! It's supposed to bring an adventure." He added one last grunt.

Elizabeth shook her head slowly. "Jonathan? Why are you so weird?"

Jonathan trotted after her as she walked to the back door. "I'm not weird. You said you were tired of playing detective. And you want a real mystery. So I'm trying to get us one."

"Get us a mystery? Here?" Elizabeth turned away and rolled her eyes. Their grandfather's roomy wooden house was about as mysterious as an old slipper. No secret chambers or trap doors. Just a plain grey two-story on a shady hill. Down below, a sunlit bay opened onto a long, deep lake, busy with boats. "Forget about grunting, Jonathan.

There's no mystery here."

"Oh, I wouldn't be so sure about that." Their mother walked from the car, looking small behind the bulky black suitcase she carried. "There *is* something about this house," said Mrs. Pollack, "but ... I haven't thought about it for a long time." She stopped by the back door. Her brown eyes squinted up toward the sky, as if she were trying to see something very far away. "You know the old portrait. The one that hangs in the living room. I used to think that was very mysterious."

"What do you mean?" Elizabeth had never paid much attention to the painting. She could vaguely remember a man with a long beard and unfriendly eyes.

"I know! It's the beard!" Jonathan began dancing around the birdbath again. "I bet the beard in the picture is growing. It's getting longer and longer. It's going to grow right out of the frame. It's going to start creeping across the room and wrapping around people's legs. And ... and there's probably some kind of family curse. Right?"

Mrs. Pollack laughed. "Well, nothing quite like that. Just a family story. Let's see. According to the story, my great-grandmother Lydia talked about that painting just before she died. She kept saying it should never, *ever* be sold or given away. She made the whole family give a solemn promise. As if the painting was very important or had some kind of secret."

Elizabeth reached out as Mrs. Pollack opened the screen door. "Mom, wait! Didn't you ever look for the secret?"

"I did try once. Come to think of it, I must have been about eleven years old. Exactly your age, Elizabeth. I remember climbing up on a chair and looking over the whole painting with a magnifying glass. I didn't find any secret though. I don't think anybody else did either. Anyway, you can ask Pop about it."

"Ask Pop? Well, uh, maybe you should ask him."

Jonathan nodded. Pop was not a cozy, storybook kind of

grandfather. He was grumpy and hard, like a table with sharp corners. Especially since Gran died.

Elizabeth and Jonathan let their mother go in first. They followed her into a large, creaky kitchen, with a scuffed wooden floor and blue flowers fading on the wallpaper. Pop was nowhere to be seen.

Elizabeth stood in the middle of the room and closed her eyes. Her detective handbook said people use their eyes too much. A good detective had to feel and hear and smell, not just see. With her eyes still shut, Elizabeth concentrated on Pop's kitchen. Cigar smoke. A hint of bacon grease and hot dogs. And a wheezy hum from the old round-shouldered refrigerator.

"Hey, Mom, guess what! Elizabeth is in a … in a … trance." Jonathan snapped his fingers in front of her face. "You will now wake up and start clucking like a chicken."

"Jonathan, leave me alone. I'm trying to practice my detective skills." Elizabeth lifted her head and gave the air an expert sniff. "Pop had bacon for breakfast, broiled hot dogs for lunch, smoked a cigar, and then …" She heard long, slow snores, trembling in the air like distant thunder. "And then he went into the den to take a nap."

Mrs. Pollack set down her suitcase. "Okay, Sherlock Holmes. Let's go see if you're right."

* * *

Elizabeth stayed in the doorway with Jonathan. Their grandfather snored softly, his face half buried in a pillow. Elizabeth could see one sandpaper cheek, grey and wrinkled, like the bark of a very old tree. And just above him—something new. Pop's collection of wooden masks had come out of the trunk. They hung scowling on the wall now. Fierce-looking faces with empty eyes and open mouths.

"Dad, we're here." Mrs. Pollack placed a slender hand on her father's shoulder. Pop straightened up stiffly, smoothing back a few thin grey hairs. "Well?" His voice erupted in a low rumble. "What do you do when you see your grandfather?" After receiving brief pecks on the cheek, he squinted at Elizabeth. "What happened to your hair?"

Elizabeth straightened her glasses and tucked a loose strand of hair behind her ear. She could feel her long ponytail drooping like a wilted flower.

"Elizabeth looks just fine, Dad." Mrs. Pollack spoke a little sharply. "We've been in the car all day, and it's very hot outside."

Elizabeth glanced at Jonathan. *His* hair looked like the day after a tornado. "Where's your cat, Pop?" Jonathan dropped to the floor, out of Pop's view. He stuck his head underneath the couch. "And what's her name? I forgot."

"She doesn't have a name. I just call her Cat." Pop lifted himself off the couch. "Don't bother about the cat. She doesn't like children. Anyway, I want to give you two a test. To see how observant you are."

A test? During summer vacation? Elizabeth and Jonathan shuffled into the living room behind Pop. The wide picture window showed two sailboats skimming across the lake. The silky blue water looked warm. Perfect for swimming.

"Pay attention!" Pop banged three times on a long marble coffee table. "I want you to tell me what's missing. Right there." He pointed to the dark-paneled wall, just above a stiff black couch.

Elizabeth turned around and looked up. "Oh, no! The picture of the man with the beard is gone! Mom was just telling us about it."

"Not *picture*. It's a *painting*—a portrait of my great-grandfather, Joshua Bailey." Elizabeth and Jonathan exchanged glances.

"You didn't sell it, did you?" asked Jonathan. "You aren't supposed to."

"Of course I didn't sell it. The frame needed to be fixed. I sent the painting to a place in Walworth." Pop wagged a thin finger at Jonathan. "You have to take care of old family things. Keep them fixed up. Of course, no one cares about old things any more."

"Mom cares about old things," said Elizabeth. "She teaches history, and she—"

"Computers!" Pop spit the word out like poison. "That's all people care about. Or watching television. Idiot box! That's what I call it!" He was interrupted by the jangle of the telephone.

Pop answered with an irritated *Hello.* "I can't hear you! I'm eighty-one years old. You have to speak up." He paused, then thrust the telephone into Elizabeth's hands. "It's Mr. Lattimore. The man who's repairing the frame. See what he wants. I can't hear him."

"But, Pop, I … don't you think Mom should talk?" It was no use. Mrs. Pollack was outside unpacking the car. Jonathan edged away, suddenly interested in Pop's travel souvenirs. He picked up a long brass elephant prod from the coffee table.

When the conversation was over, Elizabeth was still gripping the telephone receiver. "He said we can pick up the painting. As long as we get there before five o'clock." She looked up as her mother walked into the room. "But it's kind of strange. Mr. Lattimore said he found something … mysterious when he took off the frame."

"What did he find?" Jonathan struck a heroic pose with the elephant prod.

"He didn't say. He said he'd show us when we get there." Elizabeth stared at the empty spot on the wall. The secret of the old portrait. Mr. Lattimore must have found it.

Jonathan hung on his mother's arm. "We can pick it up today, can't we? And find out about the mystery?"

* * *

Elizabeth ignored the tidy farmhouses and sleepy-looking cows. She imagined a stormy sky and dark castles on the horizon. And herself, of course. The world's most famous eleven-year-old detective. She closed her eyes, letting Mr. Lattimore's words slide into her mind. *I found something when I took off the frame. Something… mysterious.*

138

Books of Interest

Eleanor Florence Rosellini

Also by Eleanor Rosellini, an excerpt from *The Mystery of the Ancient Coins ...*

The Mystery Letter

"Jonathan, you are so disgusting!" Elizabeth Pollack, ace detective, stood in her grandfather's living room on a snow-covered December morning. She glared at her younger brother, whose nose was deeply buried in a box of chocolates. Jonathan blissfully sniffed his way down the first row of candies, like a bee flitting from flower to flower.

"Get your nose out of there, Jon. You're slobbering all over the candy."

"I'm not slobbering." Jonathan straightened up to his full height—a skinny four feet, three inches. "You said I'm supposed to practice being a detective. So I'm training my nose. I can tell if a piece has vanilla or raspberry filling, just by smelling. Then I dig a hole in the bottom and see if I'm right. Great, huh?" Jonathan hung his chunky front teeth over his lower lip and rolled his eyeballs back. It was his latest trick. Goof smile with zombie eyes. He snapped his face back to normal as he popped a chocolate into his mouth. "But I wish Pop would get some chocolate-covered grasshoppers. They're even better, 'cause they're nice and crunchy."

Elizabeth didn't give Jonathan the pleasure of a grimace. He was the kind of eight-year-old brother who lived only to annoy. "You must be crazy, messing around with Pop's candy," she said. "You know he'll find out." Their grandfather, Pop, noticed everything. Way down deep, he was nice, but mostly he went through life at a low grumble. "And anyway, Jonathan, I don't think you even care about being a detective."

"Yeah? Well, if you're Miss Perfect Detective, how come you can't find that letter Pop lost?"

Elizabeth felt herself stiffen. The missing letter. It was the best—and worst—thing that had happened in months. A week before Christmas, their grandfather had received a letter in his post office box. It wasn't written to him, but instead was mysteriously addressed to *Detectives Elizabeth and Jonathan Pollack.* Pop put it in a safe place, so they would find it when they arrived for their visit. But by the time they came, Pop had forgotten where the safe place was. They searched everywhere, all the rooms, upstairs and down, and every piece of prim old furniture. Two days of hunting, and the letter was still missing.

"I just hope Pop didn't throw it away by mistake," Elizabeth said. "Things are always disappearing around here." She had never met anyone more fiercely neat than her grandfather. Pop was beyond tidy. He was at war with clutter, and his stormy clean-ups usually meant trouble. Christmas money would disappear, crumpled up with used gift wrap. Rings would be flung into the garbage, mistaken for pop-up tops from soda cans.

"Well, I don't think Pop threw it away," said Jonathan. "I bet that letter is right in this room." He peeked behind the wooden legs of a stiff, leather sofa, then shuffled through a pile of travel magazines on the coffee table.

"I don't know. It seems like we've looked everywhere." Elizabeth stared out the picture window, but she found nothing to cheer her up. The world looked as if it had been washed with a dirty rag. At the bottom of the hill the lake lay flat and dull under a sulky gray sky. Even the snow had lost its sparkle. Christmas Day had been different—full of sunshine and bright as a brass band. The house had been happy, too, almost like when Gran was alive. But then it was time for everyone to go home. Their aunt and cousins left first. Their father went back to Indiana to a teachers' meeting. Elizabeth and Jonathan stayed behind with their mother to spend a few extra days with Pop. Elizabeth didn't mind staying—except for the quiet. It drifted in as soon as the others were gone, spreading stillness through the house like a fine layer of dust.

"Okay, let's get going, Jon. Mom said we're supposed to have this place cleaned up before they get back from the store."

"I *am* cleaning up." Jonathan grabbed a wadded-up ball of gift wrap and raced twice around the coffee table. "And he dodges. He fakes. Two seconds left!" Jonathan took a long shot, tossing the gift wrap into the recycling box. "The crowd is on their feet. They never... ooh!" Jonathan winced as a dark object hit the picture window with a thud. He peered through the glass and pointed to a tiny brown sparrow lying motionless in the snow. "Look! He hurt himself on the window. And... and now he's going to get eaten." The neighbor's striped gray cat appeared suddenly, slinking across the driveway. It hunched down, like a stain against the snow, with its hard green eyes fixed on the bird.

Elizabeth didn't know Jonathan was gone until she heard the back door slam. He raced to the front of the house, sloshing through the snow in Pop's black galoshes. She ran into the kitchen and met him at the door. Jonathan held the bird cupped in his hands. Its tiny chest fluttered up and down in faint whispers of breath.

"Do you think it's going to die?" asked Jonathan softly.

"Well, it's breathing, anyway. We'll keep it in the house to warm up. Hold on. We can use the basket Mom got for Christmas." Elizabeth set a roomy wicker basket on the kitchen table. She guided Jonathan's hands as he gently set the bird inside. "He needs to rest awhile," she said. "When he wakes up we can let him go. And as long as we're using Mom's Christmas presents, we can cover up the basket with this." She picked up a square pink scarf from the sofa and draped it over the basket.

Jonathan peeked under the scarf. "I'm naming him Mugsy."

* * *

Elizabeth came up with a split-second plan. While Jonathan closed the curtains to keep the bird from hitting the window, she ran into the kitchen to get the pink scarf. She held it out in front of her, walking slowly, like a toreador approaching a bull.

"Don't worry, Mugsy. I'm just going to throw this over you and take you back outside." With the sparrow eyeing her nervously, she tossed the scarf up into the air. It floated down, empty, as the bird made an easy escape to the antlers hanging above the fireplace.

"Here. Let me do it. You gotta get wrist action." Jonathan grabbed the scarf and climbed up on a heavy chair next to the fireplace. "Three pointer!" He took aim and gave a mighty heave. The scarf ended up on the highest prong of the antlers. Mugsy flapped away and flew into a narrow den next to the living room. He headed for Pop's warrior mask collection, landing sideways on a hollow-eyed wooden face mounted on the wall.

"Hey, Elizabeth!" Jonathan, still perched on the chair, reached up behind a wooden pendulum clock on the mantel. "There's something up here." He pulled out a small white envelope propped up behind the clock. "The mystery letter!" He waved the paper in the air.

"Great. But forget it for now!" yelled Elizabeth. "Mugsy just flew in the den. And he ... Not again!" Elizabeth groaned as she spotted a white splat on Pop's antique desk. "This is it, Jonathan! Bread and water for us!"

Elizabeth shot into the den and yanked the door shut. The wooden mask fell off the wall and crashed behind the couch. Mugsy fluttered away and sank his claws into a clump of hairy strings hanging from another mask. Elizabeth pressed her lips together and looked desperately around the room. The scarf idea would never work, but ... the window. They were in luck. The den had an old crank window with no screen. Elizabeth used two hands to creak it open. A blast of cold air scattered the papers on Pop's desk. "Okay, Mugsy. This is your chance." She clapped her hands sharply and the bird took off again. This time it flew in a straight line out the window. "Jon, you can come in now." She lunged forward and cranked the window shut.

The two crowded up against the glass. Mugsy didn't stay around long. He flew up into a pine tree, pecked at his feathers indignantly, then flew away.

"Now, *that* was weird." Elizabeth sank into the soft cushions of Pop's old red couch. "The letter!" She bounced off as if she had sat on a thumb tack. "Where did you put the letter?"

"I left it up there." Standing in front of the fireplace, Jonathan stretched up and slipped the small envelope off the mantel. This was the mystery letter. No doubt about it. Their names were scrawled across the front. *Detectives Elizabeth and Jonathan Pollack.* The writing was odd, somehow—bold and yet shaky at the same time. As Jonathan tore open the envelope, Elizabeth looked up at the old pendulum clock. Usually she barely noticed its gentle sound, but now each tick sounded as sharp as the crack of a whip, as if the clock were hurrying them. Urging them on.

Jonathan pulled out a small sheet of plain white paper. As he unfolded the letter, Elizabeth read over his shoulder.

Dear Elizabeth and Jonathan,

Your grandfather told me of your interest in detective work and has sent me a newspaper article about the mystery you solved last summer. Congratulations on your good work! I understand you'll be staying at your grandfather's house for a few days after Christmas. I would be delighted if you could pay me a visit.

If you still like mysteries, I think you'll be interested to hear what I have to say.

> *All the best from*
> *Poor Uncle Rudy*
> *Rudolf Obermeyer*

Elizabeth read the last sentence a second, then a third time. She had a tingly feeling, like being on a roller coaster just before it starts zooming downhill. She thought about last summer, when the old portrait on Pop's wall led them to a family secret and a long-forgotten mystery. Ever since then, Elizabeth had been waiting. She didn't know why or how, but she knew another mystery was going to find her.